The
Night
Tommy
Swanson
Died.

The Morning We Found Tommy Swanson's Body

Tommy Swanson was the boy who always cut the neighborhood lawns in the summer. He had bad acne all over his face and back, but he still took his shirt off when he cut lawns anyway. Whenever he was cutting mine, I'd watch him from my bedroom window and try to hide if he ever looked up. I made it into a game. I think he saw me, once or twice, but he just smiled and pretended that he didn't so I could keep playing.

I didn't know Tommy very well, but I always wished that I did. I feel like he would've liked me. Maybe we could've been friends somehow if things were different and I were older, or maybe if he were younger.

In the summer that my grandpa got sick, Tommy hanged himself from the monkey bars on the playground across the street. Mrs. Turner was the first to find him in the morning. Midway through her jog, she saw his body swinging from the monkey bars like the pendulum of a grandfather clock. She didn't scream when she found him because she didn't believe it at first.

I didn't either. I was young back then, only nine-years-old. The entire neighborhood had gathered around the playground because there were a lot of sirens and flashing lights. I saw one of the older boys, Harold, barefoot and wearing rocket ship pajamas that were probably two sizes too small. Normally, he would never let any of us see him like that, but today was different because something was happening. I didn't quite know what it was, but I could tell that it was bad because everything kind of stopped for a while.

Before the police cut down the rope, the news truck came by. A balding man stormed out of the passenger side and snapped a few photographs that made it onto the front page of the paper. The next day, when the paperboy rode by on his bicycle, he tossed the small, rolled up bundle between the sweating milk bottles that stood on the front porch like bowling pins. The photo of Tommy was blurry and dark, but when I squinted hard, I could see the nail polish on his fingers. I think about that, sometimes. That was the strangest part about that morning.

Tommy had painted his nails green. Somebody down the street told us that Tommy had taken his younger sister's nail polishes and mixed the blues and the yellows and used that to color in his nails. Afterward, he dumped it all down the front of his white t-shirt. In the light of the rising sun, those green splatters looked like vomit.

"Give us some damn *space!*" one of the policemen griped, herding the crowd of onlookers away from the playground. "Nothing to see here!"

"I… I saw him blink!" one of the boys beside me hollered. He pointed frantically toward Tommy Swanson, or at least, what was left of him. "Didn't you see? He… he *winked* at us!"

"He couldn't have," another boy whispered, taking a bite out of a candy bar and then talking with a mouthful of chocolate. "Before the cops came, I poked him with a stick and he didn't move. He wasn't even breathing."

I was about to ask him what Tommy's eyes looked like because he had died with his eyes open and I was too far away to see them, but before I could ask, I was interrupted by the policeman, who'd moved so close to us that I could feel the spit from his lips.

"Move back!" he demanded, his voice straining. "Nothing to see here!"

But there *was* something to see. At least, I thought so. My eyes were wide and filled with wonder, and even though he was forcing us back, I tried to push my way to the front of the crowd so I could see it all.

A few policemen cut down the rope with a pair of hedge clippers. When Tommy hit the ground, his body made a dull thud and a few men pulled off his shirt so the kids wouldn't see the color on it.

"Move *back*!" came the policeman's voice again. We tried to. Somebody stepped on my foot and I yelped and accidentally closed my teeth overtop my tongue. The warm taste of blood filled my mouth and I spat out ropes of saliva that had red in them.

"Sorry," the boy beside me mumbled, staring at the glob of saliva that had fallen at our feet. It was cloudy and seemed to bubble on the hot sidewalk like an egg on a frying pan.

"You stepped on my foot!" I cried, wiping my mouth and then trying to shove the boy out of the way.

Just then, a gust of wind whistled across the playground and hundreds of red petals from the apple trees danced through the air. For a moment, we were all so distracted by how pretty it looked that we forgot where we were and what we were looking at. When the air became clear again, we all grew frightened because Tommy Swanson's head was facing us and it looked like he was watching everybody watching him.

And I could've sworn I saw him wink.

"He... he winked!" I breathed, but I could barely choke it out before I started to cry. That was the hardest I'd ever cried and I didn't even know why I was doing it. I couldn't stop for hours, even after Tommy Swanson was taken away and everybody went home and I was sitting in the den watching *Leave It To Beaver* with my family.

I don't remember much more about that summer, just that our grass grew really long once or twice and tickled my ankles. Apart from that, I remember the carnival. When the neighborhood boys whispered to one another and the housewives gossiped through the telephone wires that crackled above our heads, one thing was always taken as undeniable truth.

The carnival was the last place Tommy Swanson had gone before he died.

I never understood why he wanted to die that day, no matter how hard I tried. On nights that I couldn't fall asleep because I was thinking too much about him, I imagined that things would have been different if he had gone to the carnival with me. Some nights, I even dreamt about it.

My dreams always started the same. I'd be laughing with him and playing that dumb old game where you have to toss rings around empty root beer bottles. After we ran out of quarters, we would go into one of the tents and give each other noogies and look really hard and long at one another in the funhouse mirrors. Once or twice, we even pressed our hands against the fingerprinted glass and realized that we could step through the mirrors and run away to a different place where Tommy Swanson never had to leave.

But those were only dreams and Dad told me that dreams were silly, so I stopped dreaming them after a while.

On the last night of Barnaby's Carnival, three days after Tommy Swanson was taken away, I watched the fireworks from outside my bedroom window. Back then, the carnival used to give out free hotdogs and everyone would drive to the big field next to the carnival and park their red Chevy cars. From there, they'd watch the fireworks fill the sky with beautiful lights in celebration of the boys and girls whose childhood ended that year. It's sad that Tommy missed them. They were so beautiful that night— the red and green fireworks.

I normally went to see them with my family, but that year, my mother had a summer cold and my father was watching a boxing match on television. I heard him shouting and slamming his fist against the wall. Sometimes, his drunken cusses startled me and made me think that he was a bad person.

So when the sound of the first firework rattled the picture frames in the hallway, I climbed out of my bedroom window and sat on the small bit of roof. I could hear the crickets between the fireworks, which were bursting just above the tiny silhouette of the Ferris Wheel.

Boom! Boom!

And as I watched, for the first time in my life, I prayed outside of church. I never told anybody about what I prayed for that night. I used to be afraid people would laugh at me if I did, but I don't care about that anymore. I'm just worried that they won't understand. Sometimes, I don't even understand. It was a terribly strange thing to do, I know that, but I felt like I needed to.

So that night, I bowed my head, squeezed my eyes shut and prayed that Tommy Swanson could see the fireworks from wherever he was. Could he see them— the green fireworks? Or was he too far away?

The Night We Saw Tommy Swanson's Ghost

Brendan was the boy who lived on the other side of the neighborhood. His dad owned the lawn business that Tommy Swanson worked for before he died. Brendan's house smelled like fertilizer and there were always a few clumps of grass on the living room carpet because they had fallen off of his father's socks.

Brendan was my best friend and we would play games and run through the sprinkler even when it was cloudy outside. He had a big backyard, much bigger than mine, and his didn't have that lumpy old tree that mine had.

The day I met Brendan, we went to the playground and played basketball and cried when the older boys stole our ball. It was a long time ago, so long ago that I hardly remember it. Brendan used to wear tank tops and thonged sandals, so the older boys made fun of him.

"Hey, fairies don't play ball!" they cackled. One of them was big and we were afraid of him. He smelled like fish and had a lot of stains on his shirt.

"Give it back!" I cried. "Or… or we'll tell…"

"Tell? Tell who?"

I opened my mouth to respond, but nothing came out. The boys called us more names and tossed our ball into the bushes. When we finally managed to fish it out, it didn't bounce anymore because there was a hole in it somewhere.

A few days later, we snuck into our neighbor's yard when everybody was asleep and broke all of the garden gnomes. The older boys got into trouble for it and we laughed.

"What do you think it will be like when we're finally grown up?" Brendan asked me one day, the summer after Tommy Swanson died. We were lying on the hill in his backyard and staring up at clouds.

I shrugged. My eyes traced the outline of one particular cloud, which was the largest in the sky. Back then, the clouds still made shapes when I looked at them.

I lowered my eyes. "It'll be wonderful, won't it? I'll be just like Dad."

When I looked over at Brendan, I saw his eyes following the passing clouds, too. I wondered what shapes he saw.

After a minute or two of silence, he sat up. A few blades of grass fell from his back. "Do we have to be?"

My forehead crinkled a bit because I didn't understand. "What do you mean?"

"Do we have to be like them? Our dads?"

I went silent and thought about it harder. "I guess not. We can be whoever we want to be. That's what's so great about it."

Once Brendan thought about it long enough, he laid back down and watched the sky.

"Why don't you want to be like your dad?" I asked, suddenly curious because Brendan's dad always looked strong and always wore expensive shirts. I couldn't imagine why Brendan wouldn't want to be like him.

Brendan didn't answer me right away because he was thinking again. "I don't like his job. It must be so boring."

I leaned forward. "Boring? No way! I'd like it. It'd be easy, wouldn't it? To just paint grass all day long. You start in the front yard in the morning and work your way to the back. Then, before you know it, the whole thing's red."

"It's harder than it seems," Brendan said, twirling a blade of grass between his fingers. "I helped my dad once with Mrs. Trammel's yard. My hands got really bad blisters and they were stained red for days, even after I kept washing them."

"I bet the grass looked really good, though. Besides, his job is important because nobody wants green grass anymore. It makes you look poor. It's funny, though. Your dad paints grass for a living, but your grass is still green."

Brendan watched me tug at a hunk of green grass.

"He says he doesn't like all the chemicals. They make him cough."

"Cough?"

"Yeah, and it takes him a long time to stop sometimes."

"Oh, I guess I never really thought about that..."

I fell silent and so did Brendan, who sighed and placed his hands on his chest and continued watching the clouds. Just to mess with him, I grabbed my throat and pretended to cough really loudly like I was choking. He was suddenly alarmed and I rolled over and played dead. When he finally understood, he laughed and jumped on top of me.

It's strange to think about that day now, because neither of us knew it at the time, but less than two years later, Brendan's dad was going to cough and blood was going to come out and he'd be dead before Brendan's fourteenth birthday.

But that was in the future, and the future was still our friend, so that day, we laughed and rolled around and didn't talk about growing up anymore.

* * * * *

A few days later, the older boys dared me and Brendan to go to the playground after dark. They said that it was haunted by the ghost of Tommy Swanson. They told us that he swings from the monkey bars at midnight and laughs and never gets any older.

"He's gonna be naked," one of them said while another nodded, "because the cops took his clothes off after he died because they were all

9

green. All that he wears now is a clown mask with a red nose and droopy eyes."

We didn't believe them, so we snuck out of our houses at eleven thirty and hurried over to the playground. I told Brendan to bring a basketball so we could play while we waited. I knew that Brendan was afraid because he kept looking at the monkey bars the entire night. I tried to distract him by telling him the story of the day that my mom backed over the neighbor's cat with our car, but he wasn't listening. Annoyed, I tossed the ball at him.

"Come on, Brendan," I said, watching it roll between his legs. He didn't even notice.

"Do you hear something?"

I listened, but couldn't hear anything. "All that I hear is your breathing. They made that whole thing up to scare us. Tommy's dead. He's not coming back."

Brendan swallowed hard. "I know he's dead, but what if he's still here? He could be watching us like an... an *angel* or something."

"Why would he do that? There are roller coasters and all kinds of better stuff to do in heaven. He'd be a fool to come back here."

"We have roller coasters, too. Don't we?"

"Not ones that are a thousand feet tall. You can't trust what the older boys say, okay? Don't be stupid."

Brendan pulled his gaze from the monkey bars. When his eyes met mine, they narrowed. "Don't say that. I'm not *stupid.*"

I bit my bottom lip, surprised that he had gotten angry because he normally wouldn't have. "Sorry," I said quickly. "I know you're not stupid. You're the smartest kid I know. I just don't want you to believe those guys."

Brendan's face softened a bit. "No kidding? Am I really the smartest kid you know?"

"Of course," I sighed. "You got the brains and I got the good looks. Okay?"

A smile spread across his face. He picked up the ball and tossed it at me. I laughed and swatted it away and we went back to playing basketball for a few minutes until Brendan's watch beeped.

"Midnight," he whispered.

"It looks like we made it after all. See? I told you they were pulling your leg."

He puffed out his chest. "Yeah, I'm never believing anything they say again."

We started to head home a few moments later. As I was showing Brendan the stars that made up Orion's belt, we heard a loud snap from behind.

And that's when we saw him.

A boy was hurrying across the basketball court. He was very far away, shrouded in darkness, but I could still tell that he was naked apart from a white mask that he was wearing to cover his face. When he finally reached the monkey bars, he jumped up and grabbed hold of them.

I heard Brendan gasp and nearly fall backward. "Do you.... see that?" he asked me, his voice shaky.

I nodded, but I couldn't find my voice to respond.

The two of us just watched in silence as the ghost of Tommy Swanson swung back and forth from the monkey bars. The ghost laughed while he swung— quietly, and that was what scared me the most.

When I took a step back because I was afraid, the basketball slipped from my hand and the sound of it bouncing off the macadam made Tommy Swanson turn to face us.

I wished I could've seen his eyes— to see if he was happy or mad. The clown mask covered his face and for a moment or two, I could've sworn that it wasn't a mask at all.

11

After several moments of silence, Tommy let go of the bars. His bare feet hit the mulch and he just stood there, motionless, staring back at us.

"Hunter… let's go…" Brendan whispered, but I didn't move because I couldn't. The hairs on my arms rose and fell like corn stalks in the wind.

Once the feeling returned to my legs, I found myself walking across the basketball court toward the monkey bars. I'm not really sure why, but I wanted to ask Tommy what he saw that night at the carnival because I needed to know what happened the night Tommy Swanson died.

Even when Brendan hissed my name, I kept walking. The only thing that made me stop was the terrible scream.

Tommy began to shout and grab hold of his neck like he was in a lot of pain. After a few moments, he began sprinting toward us. We shouted in fear and stumbled over one another. Brendan fell first. His knee skidded on the cement court and he cried out. I tripped too, but my palms broke my fall.

Just then, we heard laughter. Several of the older boys came out from behind the bushes. The boy with the clown mask, the one we'd thought was Tommy Swanson, pulled off the mask and threw it onto the ground before us. I recognized him as Michael Evans, a boy from my school who had buzzed hair and the features of a rat. His eyes were wide, as if he were surprised that we had gotten scared.

"They told me to do it," he whispered, almost apologetically. "They told me it'd be funny."

"Did you piss yourself?" came a voice from over our shoulders. It belonged to one of the older boys— the one that smelled like fish.

We didn't answer. The older boys tossed Michael a pair of shorts and he quickly pulled them on as if he'd been embarrassed to be seen naked. Once finished, Michael followed the other boys as they laughed their way down the street and out of sight.

"That was a cruel prank," I said to Brendan.

But Brendan wasn't listening. He kept exhaling between clenched teeth while gripping his knee. It was bleeding pretty badly. There were a few pieces of gravel stuck to it. I outstretched a hand to help him up, but he didn't take it, so instead, I knelt down beside him.

"Does it hurt badly?" I asked.

He nodded.

Without thinking twice, I leaned forward and kissed the top of his knee, just above the scrape, like my mother always used to do. Then, I leaned back and said, "There, it'll start feeling better soon. Okay?"

And when I looked into Brendan's eyes, he smiled and his tears went away.

The Day Gabriel Turned Thirteen

Gabriel was Brendan's older brother. He laughed at us the night that we thought we saw a ghost on the playground. Two summers after Tommy Swanson died, he started cutting the neighborhood lawns, but I didn't watch him out of the window like I watched Tommy Swanson because I felt too old to be doing that. I saw Gabriel with stained hands once or twice when I was playing at Brendan's. I knew they were stained because he had been helping his father paint peoples' front lawns red.

Even though he had a job and was older, Gabriel always liked Brendan and me. He apologized, once, for scaring us the summer before. He said that he only laughed at us because the other boys were laughing and he didn't know what else to do.

Gabriel turned thirteen the summer that he started cutting lawns, which was the first summer that nobody really talked about Tommy Swanson anymore because he was old news. I was only eleven that year, and Brendan was still ten because his birthday wasn't until a few weeks after Gabriel's.

Gabriel invited me to his birthday party, but only so that Brendan would have somebody to play with. The party was held inside this little skating rink called *Skate Away*. His mother hung decorations all over the rink that said, "LUCKY NUMBER 13" and "THANK YOU FOR SHARING MY FINAL DAYS OF CHILDHOOD WITH ME."

Before the party, Brendan's mom fussed and made a big deal out of everything. Gabriel fussed, too. They all wanted everything to be perfect. I understood why. I knew that thirteenth birthdays meant the end of childhood. When I saw all of the balloons and wrapped presents at the party, I was jealous that his childhood got to end and mine didn't.

When Brendan's mother finally shouted, "Time for presents!" we all sat down to watch Gabriel open a set of red boxing gloves. I knew

14

that they were expensive because I remembered seeing them in the store window when I went shopping one day with my mom.

"We wanted to get him something special," I heard his mother saying later that night when I was trying to pour myself some cola. "It's the least we can do. It comes so fast, doesn't it? Our little boys are growing up."

The other woman, Mrs. Samuelson, nodded. "It's nice that you bought him something special before.... well... *it* happens."

"I just hope he likes them."

"Oh, don't be silly. He's a little boy. You know how they are. You won't be able to get those gloves off of him— not even to eat!"

They chuckled and then continued to talk about things that I didn't understand, but I do remember curiosity igniting somewhere inside of me because Mrs. Samuelson said "it" like it was a bad thing. Her voice had fallen to a whisper, like she was whispering profanity, and she winced slightly.

"I wonder what *it* is," I said to Brendan, moments later, while we were playing pinball near the snack bar.

"It's the end of childhood. That's why this party is so big and special."

"I know childhood ends at thirteen," I said, "but I always thought it was a good thing. You should've heard Mrs. Samuelson. The way she said it was... *different*. I got nervous when I heard it. What if they know something that we don't? What if Gabriel should be worried?"

Brendan shrugged. "The last time I talked to Gabriel, he said that it wasn't a big deal. Mom was just fussing and it was making him fuss, too."

I sighed. "Yeah, but you know Gabriel. He doesn't get worried easily and even if he did, he wouldn't tell you."

"I know he wouldn't, but I'm his brother. I can tell when he's worried and he seems really excited— especially for the fireworks. They're for him this year because his childhood is ending."

I imagined the green fireworks exploding in the night sky beneath the moon and between all the stars. My eyes must've grown really wide thinking about that. "Say..." I whispered, smiling at the thought. "We should watch them together this year. It'll be the first time, won't it?"

Brendan thought about it for a moment. "Yeah, I'd like that," he said, turning to face me. I'm not sure if he realized how close his lips came to mine, but in that moment, for the first time in my life, I wanted to kiss him. I didn't know how to kiss, because I was so young and I'd never done it before, but I wanted to try it with him because the thought of that seemed really nice.

I wondered if Brendan was thinking the same thing because we both just stood there, staring into one another's eyes until we heard a loud cry from beside us.

The pinball machine lit up with "GAME OVER." I laughed and gave Brendan a noogie and we didn't talk about the fireworks or the end of childhood anymore. Instead, we kept eating popcorn and playing pinball because we knew that our childhood wasn't going to end for another two years, and for some reason, we felt like that day would never come.

* * * * *

I saw Gabriel a few days after his party when I went over to play at Brendan's house. He wore those bright red boxing gloves the entire time that Brendan and I were running around the backyard. Even though I'd forgotten about most of his party, I was still thinking about Mrs.

Samuelson's face when she said "it" and how her body seemed to shudder.

I asked Gabriel what "it" was while he punched at his bed posts later that day. We didn't normally go into Gabriel's room because he didn't like having us in there, but I wanted to know if there was something more to growing up— something that nobody ever told me.

"What did she say again?" he asked me after I'd told him about Mrs. Samuelson.

"She said that your boxing gloves were something special given to you before 'it' happens. What did she mean? What's 'it'?"

Gabriel shrugged. "All of the moms just get sad when their kids grow up, that's all."

I looked him up and down. He didn't look grown-up to me. He still played on the playground and jumped on the bed when his mother wasn't home.

"You don't look like a grown up yet," I said. "You still look like one of us."

"Because I'm not grown up *yet*," he told me.

"But you're thirteen."

"Your childhood doesn't end on your thirteenth birthday, Hunter. It ends when you finally… *see* it."

Gabriel didn't wince when he said "it" like Mrs. Samuelson.

"See what?"

He smirked. "You really don't know how it happens, do you?"

I shook my head. "Nobody tells me anything. They say I'm too young."

He leaned in further. "No kidding? You don't know how childhood ends?"

"No. I just know about the parties and the carnival with the fireworks. I know it all celebrates the end of childhood. I just don't know what changes. Why do you get to grow up, and I don't?"

"The carnival isn't a celebration. The fireworks are, but the carnival isn't."

I looked over at Brendan, who shrugged and looked just as confused as me.

"It's not?" we asked together.

"No. The carnival is just the place where it happens."

"Where *what* happens?" I asked, impatient, because I was sick of hearing the word "it" because *it* just made everything more confusing.

"*Christ*," Gabriel sighed. "The carnival is where everybody's childhood ends. They say that it's the best place to say goodbye to those days. Every year, all the thirteen-year-olds pay two quarters to go to the fair. And every year, they're all shown something before they leave that makes them grow up, right there on the spot."

I tried really hard to think of what that could be, but all that I could think about were the monkeys that ate bananas from your hands and all the pretty lights of the rides.

"But I've gone to the carnival with my family and I've never seen anything that made me grow up."

His smirk widened and he pulled off his gloves and threw them on the bed. "That's because it's hidden in the darkness of one of the tents— the biggest one of all. They call it the Freak Tent, and I don't know what's in there, but my friend has an older sister who knows and she said... she said that locked inside that tent are..."

His voice trailed to silence. I crept forward.

"What's locked inside?"

"All of the monsters of the world."

And before I could even respond, Gabriel grabbed me by the hand and pulled me over to his bedroom window. He pointed into the distance, where I could see the playground through the gap between two houses. It was dark, but the street lamps illuminated the set of bars.

"Didn't you ever wonder why he did it? He was thirteen, wasn't he?"

I swallowed hard. "You mean Tommy?"

"Remember the color that he painted his nails?"

"They were green, I think."

"Tell me, what are the colors of the rainbow? What did they teach you in school?"

I began to recite them, although I wasn't sure why. "Red, orange, yellow, blue, indigo, violet..."

He nodded. "It's strange, don't you think? We paint our grass red and sometimes, when I look up in the sky after it rains, I swear that I see green up there."

"I've never seen green in the sky, except for the fireworks."

"Once you grow up, you aren't allowed to watch the green fireworks anymore."

"You're not?"

He shook his head. "Grass is meant to be green, but we make it red, and we have to close our eyes during the green fireworks and then, one day, Tommy paints his nails green and… well, you know...."

I went quiet.

"Tommy was strange. He didn't laugh when the other boys did and he always walked around like he was afraid of something. I guess he was afraid of growing up."

Gabriel made a motion with his fingers to mimic the swinging motion that Tommy made when he was hanging from the monkey bars.

"But it happens to everybody," he whispered. "And besides, I'm not afraid of growing up. I'm excited. They say that some people scream when their childhood ends, but I'm going to be ready."

"I wonder why Tommy wasn't ready. He always cut my lawn. I'd watch him from my window and try to hide when he looked up…"

"My mom says that Tommy wasn't right in the head."

19

I felt my voice rise in anger. "No. He cut the lawns all of the time. I saw him. He always seemed okay to me."

"Just look at what he did to his shirt, " Gabriel said, letting the blinds close. "He poured that green stuff all over it. Mom says that nobody in their right mind would've done that..."

I didn't answer. Too angry to stop myself, I started hitting Gabriel because he was ruining Tommy Swanson. He was making the memory of him all confused and suddenly, I didn't want to know anything more about the night Tommy Swanson died.

So instead, I kept punching Gabriel's arms until my knuckles hurt. Since he was much bigger, and didn't realize that I was mad, he grabbed his gloves and we tussled for a bit while he laughed and I almost cried.

The Day I Saw Tommy Swanson On The Playground

Another week had passed since Gabriel's party, and Brendan and I decided to have a lemonade stand. My mom was having friends over that day— all of the women that she used to read books with. I remember seeing our next-door neighbor, Mrs. Roberts, sitting in the living room. I was confused as to why she was there because my mother never spoke fondly of her. The only time that my mother ever went next door was to help Mr. Roberts clean a stain off of the dining room rug because Mrs. Roberts was busy helping with the church bake sale and he didn't want the stain to set.

"Hello, Hunter," she said cheerfully when I entered the room. Then, she winked at me.

I wasn't sure what to say back to her, since I didn't know her well, so I didn't say anything at all. Instead, Brendan and I quietly followed my mother into the kitchen so she could help us make the pitcher of lemonade. My dad tried to help us instead of my mom, because she was walking funny from her wine, but she just shooed him away. Once she was done adding the sugar and squeezing the lemons into the water, she finished by pouring a few droplets of red dye into the pitcher.

"Make sure you stir it well. Don't let it settle."

I watched the red food coloring cloud the lemonade like blood in a swimming pool.

"Mom?"

"Yes?"

"Next time, can we make the lemonade green?"

She laughed. "Lemons aren't green, honey."

I frowned. "They aren't red either…"

But she didn't hear me because she'd already returned to the den with her glass of wine and she and the other women began talking about books.

Brendan and I dragged a folding table out of the garage and propped it up at the end of the driveway. Brendan had already drawn a sign that said, "LEMONADE— $0.25 A CUP," so we taped it to the front of the table and then I brought a radio outside that I found in the attic.

While we waited for cars, we listened to music, which sounded really pretty that day for some reason, and tried to make shapes out of the clouds, but it wasn't as easy as it was before because every time I tried to make shapes of them, they all looked like monsters because I was too worried about what Gabriel had said about the end of childhood.

"Do you really think there are monsters inside that tent?" I asked Brendan.

He shrugged. "I don't know. I'm not sure if I believe in monsters anymore."

"Yeah," I whispered. "Me neither."

And for the next few minutes, when I looked up at the sky, I saw a cloud that looked like a heart and I could've sworn that Brendan saw it, too.

The older boys ruined it when they came by on their bicycles.

"A lemonade stand?" they chuckled darkly, and they began to ride up and down the driveway even when we told them to stop. One of the boys told us to give him a cup for free, and when we said no, he spat in the pitcher and then laughed.

Angry, I grabbed hold of the handlebars of his bike and tried to push him over, but he just laughed harder because he was stronger and older.

I'm not sure why, but I suddenly wanted to hurt him, and my eyes flashed over to the playground and I thought about the end of childhood.

"I bet you're not going to be so tough in a few days!" I spat. "You act so tough now, but you'll be sorry!"

The laughter left his lips. "What did you say?"

"You're not going to be laughing when you have to go inside that stupid tent! But I will! I'll be laughing when *you're* scared this time!"

"What do you know about any of that?" he demanded. "I'm not going to be scared! Only girls get scared!"

"Yes you will!" I shouted back. "I bet you're going to scream and cry when your childhood ends! You turned thirteen this year, didn't you? And the carnival's coming in just a few days! That means… it means…."

"You better shut your mouth—"

I forced a laugh. "And when it does, you're going to go crying back to your mom! And maybe if we're lucky, we'll wake up and find… find *you* on the playground—"

Whack! I felt something hard collide with the side of my face. I'm not really sure what happened, but I remember Brendan shouting in fright as I fell backward. The boy who hit me, the one who spat in the lemonade, took off down the street on his bike and all of his friends followed.

"Hunter! Hunter!"

I couldn't see anything right away, just a cloudy darkness. I could still hear the older boys riding down the street and Brendan shouting my name.

But when the cloudy darkness started to fade, I saw somebody on the playground that made me want to cry. It was only for a moment while I regained my eyesight and started to feel my arms and legs again.

Why did I see him? Why was Tommy Swanson swinging on the swings?

23

"Hunter! Are you okay?" I heard Brendan ask while I struggled to sit up.

"I'm... okay," I breathed.

"He shouldn't have hit you! You should tell your mom! She'll get him into trouble!"

Suddenly, I could feel myself becoming really hot. As the tears began to bubble up in my eyes, I stormed up the front yard and into the house.

All of the women were still in the den, laughing and talking about their books. When they saw me come in, one of them joked, "Looks like we have visitors! Here to talk about the books?"

My mom rose from her seat. "Did you two make some money from your lemonade?"

I didn't answer. Instead, I choked out, "Why didn't you ever tell me?"

She was surprised. "What? What's the matter?"

"You never told me!" I said, tears running down my face. "You never told me about the carnival and that tent in the back!"

Her face softened. "Oh, honey," she said, and I could tell I was embarrassing her now. "You're... *bleeding*. Did you fall off your bike?"

"Why didn't you tell me how childhood ends?"

She pulled me into a frail hug that didn't make me feel any better. One of the women left the room to grab some tissues for my bloody nose. When my mom spoke again, her breath smelled funny because she had been drinking too much wine.

"I promise you'll be alright. Everyone is. Look at all of us."

My gaze slid around the room. All of the women forced smiles.

I felt my mother's warm fingers on my face. She turned my chin to face her so she could wipe away the blood. I wanted her to stop because I didn't like smelling wine on her breath, but she held my chin

24

steady. "My baby is growing up," she said, looking me up and down. "That doesn't have to be a bad thing, alright?"

I backed away. Brendan was standing behind me in the doorway and I almost tripped over him.

"But not everyone is okay after," I whispered.

"Honey, everybody grows up. It just... *happens* one day."

I swallowed hard. Then, I asked the question that worried me more than anything. I knew I shouldn't have, but I couldn't stop myself.

"What about Tommy Swanson?"

At the mention of his name, my mother's eyes grew wide, like I had said a bad word. Behind her, the other women exchanged glances.

"Tommy went inside that tent," I continued, tears bubbling up in my eyes again. "But he wasn't okay. Why not? What did he do wrong?"

The Night Gabriel Learned What's Inside The Freak Tent

I didn't get any answers from anybody. My mom bought me some ice cream that day and the other women went home early because they "didn't have any more books to talk about."

Less than one week later, the carnival rolled into town. The first night, I went with Brendan and his mom because it was Brendan's birthday. It always fell on a day that the carnival was there, and that always seemed like a good thing before, but not anymore.

His mother paid for Brendan and me to go on the Ferris Wheel that day. I remember how nice it felt when the gondola rocked to a halt at the top. I remember staring at Brendan as he smiled and peered over the side. His smile faded when he saw that large tent pitched up so high that it looked like a crouching animal waiting to pounce.

Afterward, when I was feeding one of the monkeys, I noticed another in the back of the cage that looked frail and ill. On our way to the exit, his mom bought me a caramel apple, but there was a worm inside.

And when we left and went back over to Brendan's house, I saw Gabriel and he looked different, like he hadn't gotten a lot of sleep.

"Why didn't you go with us tonight? You could've ended your childhood tonight and we would've been there for you."

He shook his head. "My friends are going into the tent with me tomorrow. They turned thirteen this year, too. Besides, I'm not afraid. I don't need anybody."

I didn't believe him.

The following day, he paced up and down the halls of his house and was really quiet. "I'm leaving for the carnival," he finally told us, which was strange because he didn't normally tell us anything at all. He came all the way out into the backyard, where Brendan and I were sitting and watching the clouds.

"Now?" we asked in unison.

He nodded. "The other boys are ready. We're meeting at the tennis courts in thirty minutes."

"Are they nervous?"

Gabriel shrugged. "I'm not sure."

"Are you?"

After thinking hard and long, he said, "I just like the way things are right now. I like the way things look, and I'm not sure if they'll look the same after my childhood ends."

* * * * *

Gabriel was gone for several hours. I imagined him laughing on the Swinging Ship and screaming on the Tilt-O-Whirl and enjoying the last bits of his childhood before he wasn't a kid anymore.

"I'm scared something will happen to you," I told him before he'd left.

"Don't be," was all that he said back before closing the front door behind him.

Brendan and I watched him from the window as he marched across the lawn like a soldier leaving for war. Eventually, we couldn't see him anymore and I was worried that I was never going to see him the same again.

After a few hours, we went to the playground because Gabriel promised to meet us there afterward. We swung on the monkey bars because we weren't scared of Tommy Swanson anymore. Besides, we could hear the laughter and cheering of the carnival in the distance and it made us feel better.

"I wonder what it'll be like when we're thirteen," I whispered. "Maybe by the time we're that old, we'll understand what's inside that tent. Maybe that's why they don't make us go until we're thirteen. We wouldn't understand it."

"Yeah," Brendan whispered. "Maybe..."

I watched a firefly flicker through the mid-summer air. Another loud burst of applause and cheering sounded from the carnival, and I looked over at Brendan, but he kept his eyes on the mulch beneath our feet.

"C'mon," I said to him. "Catch fireflies with me! There's no use sitting here and moping around like somebody *died*. It'll be fun!"

"I don't know, Hunter. I'm not in the mood."

I watched the firefly flutter away. "You're killing me, Brendan! It'll take your mind off things!"

I began to chase after it. As I did, I laughed even though I knew that I felt just as worried and frightened as Brendan.

"Don't be a slowpoke!" I shouted back at him. "I'm going to catch ten before you can even catch one!"

"Hunter," he mumbled. "I told you. I'm not in the mood."

I laughed harder and ran faster. When I turned, Brendan was still sitting on the swing. "Brendan, don't be such a—"

But I hadn't been watching where I was going and I tripped over the end of the slide and came crashing to the ground. I hadn't hurt myself, but I screamed as I fell, which I hadn't meant to. The sound of Brendan's laughter suddenly flooded throughout the playground.

"It's not funny!" I said, brushing mulch off of my shorts. "My head could've fallen off."

When I looked over to Brendan, he had risen from the swing. His laughter was becoming louder because he was now chasing after the fireflies, too. When he reached me, he brushed more mulch from the back of my shirt and, together, we jumped up and down, outstretching our hands to the sky.

"I... I got one!" I heard Brendan say. When I looked over, I saw a blinking light nestled in the palm of his hand. The firefly crawled down his arm for a short moment before we both watched it fly away.

"C'mon!" Brendan said, grabbing hold of my hand. We ran off together, leaping into the air and cupping fireflies in our hands. We hurried across the basketball court and passed that big bush that the older boys threw our ball into when we were much younger.

And that's where I heard something that I hadn't expected. It was so faint that I thought that I was imagining it at first, but when I heard it a second time, I tried to quiet Brendan because he was still laughing about the fireflies.

"Did you hear that?" I asked, turning to face him. "It sounded like... *crying.*"

Brendan brushed a firefly from his bangs. "I didn't hear anything..."

"It was over *there,*" I responded, "in those bushes."

We drew closer to them. As we did, the bushes rustled a little and we both backed away, frightened.

"What do you think it is?" Brendan asked, his breath warm on my neck.

"I don't know."

I slowly pulled back the branches. From where I stood, just beyond the leaves, I could see a sliver of red. When my eyes finally adjusted to the darkness, I saw a boy lying inside the bushes, between all of the branches and flowers.

"Hello?" I whispered, bending the branches back further. "What are you doing in here? Is this a fort or something?"

The boy let out a cry. He turned to face me, his eyes wider than the moon.

"I'm sorry," I stammered, backing away. "I didn't mean to scare you!"

29

"Oh," the boy mumbled. "It's just you."

He folded his hands together again and returned them to his chest. He turned away from us and stared up at the sky, which he could see through a few breaks in the leaves.

After a moment or two, I recognized the boy's face. *"Harold?* What are you doing in here?"

"Leave me alone."

I heard another round of cheering from the distant carnival followed by a lion's roar and I became confused and worried for Harold because I knew he had turned thirteen a few months back.

"Are you hiding in here?" I asked. "So you don't have to grow up?"

He didn't nod, but I could tell by the way he bit his lip that I was right.

"The adults will find out," I warned. "You have to go."

He continued to stare up at the sky without saying a word.

"Harold? You *have* to go," I continued. "I know it's scary, but—"

"Please," he whispered, his eyes watering. "Don't tell anybody about me."

"But Harold—"

"Go away! My parents don't know that I'm here. They think that I'm at the carnival. If you say anything to them... I'll... I'll sock you right in the *goddamn nose!"*

"I won't. I swear..."

"And I'm not scared neither, okay? Don't go telling that to the other boys. I have good reasons for not wanting to go! So just close the branches and get lost."

"Okay," I whispered, letting go of the branches. They swung closed the way my bedroom curtains used to whenever I was trying to hide from Tommy Swanson.

30

And in that moment, I couldn't help but wonder what Harold Stacy was hiding from.

Suddenly, Brendan and I both heard the sound from behind. When we looked over toward the street, we saw a boy kicking at rocks while walking with his head hung low.

"Hunter," Brendan whispered, tugging on my sleeve, "I think that's Gabriel."

I squinted, but the boy was too far away. "You think so? I can't tell."

"Gabriel?" Brendan called. "Is that you?"

There was no answer. The boy kept walking.

"I don't think that's him, Brendan. He promised he was going to meet us here."

"But I *know* that's him," Brendan said. "I can tell by the way he's walking. Gabriel! Gabriel, stop!"

And as we approached, the figure became clearer, and we both recognized Gabriel's broad shoulders.

"It's us!" Brendan called. "Stop!"

But Gabriel didn't stop and I didn't understand why until we had caught up to him. We tried pulling on the back of his shirt, but he swatted us away. For a second or two, the moonlight fell across his face, which he'd been hiding from us, and that's when we realized that he was crying.

"Gabriel…" I whispered, suddenly frightened.

I let go of his shirt. He turned away again and hurried down the street, this time faster. Brendan and I watched him go.

"Gabriel never lets us see him cry," I whispered, dumbfounded. "I didn't even think that he did that anymore."

"Whatever made him cry must have been really…"

"*Bad*," I said with a slight wince.

We both stood there in silence as Gabriel's silhouette grew smaller and smaller. As I watched him go, I turned to Brendan. I was just about to invite him over to my house so we could watch cartoons and forget about Gabriel, but I knew that talking to Gabriel was the only chance I had of finding out what happened during the end of childhood.

Before Brendan could stop me, I started running after him.

"Gabriel!" I shouted. "Gabriel, wait!"

I could hear Brendan running after me. He tried to grab hold of my shirt the same way that I'd grabbed hold of Gabriel's, but I was too fast for him.

"Gabriel!" I said breathlessly, as soon as I caught up to him. I grabbed him by the hand, but this time, I wasn't going to let go.

"What is it?" I asked him. "Can you tell us what you saw?"

He didn't answer me.

"What's inside that tent?"

He turned to face me, his eyes wet with tears, and there was anger somewhere in those eyes of his, like he was suddenly jealous of me and Brendan for some reason.

"Nothing's in there," he choked. "It's all a joke. A big, *fat* joke."

He tried to leave again, but I twisted his arm.

"The adults are going to take you seriously now! Isn't that what you always wanted? How does it feel? To be grown up?"

Gabriel wiped his eyes with his free hand. "I don't... I don't *know* how it feels..."

I sighed. I was about to slacken my grip on his arm, but I saw something that made me feel sick.

"Gabriel..." I whispered. "Your hands..."

"I know!" he spat, pulling them away.

And suddenly, I became very nervous. My head became filled with all of these thoughts and suspicions, and I'm not really sure where they came from, but they frightened me.

"Your hands are all... *bloody*."

The wind rustled my hair and the breeze wrapped itself around my arms and made me shiver. The laughter and cheering of the carnival sounded so far away, like a distant dream, and I grabbed hold of Gabriel's hands even though they were sticky and red.

"Tell me what's in there," I pleaded.

His eyes darted around, searching for something that I didn't think was there. "I... I *can't*..."

"You don't have to say what you saw, but I have to know one thing..."

I pulled him closer.

"Do I need to be afraid?"

And before he ran off toward home, he whispered something that I would never forget. Right before, he gave me a long, hard look and said, "Run away, if you can."

The Night Harold Stacy Went Missing

Harold Stacy was the boy who wore the rocket ship pajamas the morning that we found Tommy Swanson's body. He didn't want to grow up because he loved wearing those and thought that he wouldn't be able to anymore. He lived a few houses down from me and sometimes waved at me when I passed his house on my way to Brendan's. Harold Stacy left the neighborhood the same summer that Gabriel turned thirteen, but not the way that Tommy Swanson had.

After I saw Gabriel return from the carnival, I began to measure the world in summers. Sometimes, I had nightmares about large spiders and black shadows crawling out of one of the carnival tents and scuttling throughout town. But worst of all, I dreamt about a pair of red eyes that loomed in the darkness in there. Sometimes, when I was awake, I saw those red eyes, too. They watched me in the mirrors and sometimes through the gap beneath the basement door.

I wondered if I should've listened to Gabriel. Should I have ran away? I could've gone into the woods or somewhere dark, where nobody could find me. I wondered what it would be like— how *good* it would feel, but I knew that no matter where I tried to hide, I wouldn't be able to escape that pair of red eyes.

"How is he doing?" I asked Brendan when we met on the playground a few nights after Gabriel had gone to the carnival. We both had climbed to the top of the fort that night. The sky was dark because the moon was only a sliver. We couldn't hear the laughter of the carnival in the distance because it had left town two days earlier.

"I don't know," he answered. "He hasn't said much. I get nervous sometimes, because all I ever hear from his room is him hitting those bedposts. He does it really late in the night sometimes."

"The boxing gloves came in handy then, didn't they?"

Brendan shook his head. "He doesn't wear those anymore."

"He doesn't?"

"He comes out of his room and his knuckles are all bloodied."

"Oh...

"Mom just says it's part of growing up."

"Yeah... I guess it is, isn't it?"

And we just sat there, staring up at the sky and thinking long and hard about the world.

"Brendan?" I whispered, after a few minutes of silence.

"Yeah?"

I took a deep breath and asked what I had been wondering for days. "Do you believe in the Devil?"

He gave me a long, hard look, but didn't say anything.

"I think I've seen him in my dreams sometimes," I continued, "in the back of that tent."

Brendan's forehead crinkled in worry and I suddenly felt guilty.

"But they're just dreams, aren't they?" I said quickly, nudging him on the shoulder.

When he didn't laugh or smile, or even tell me to "stop" when I kept nudging him, I slid down the slide. Then, I ushered for Brendan to do the same. When he finally did, I tackled him to the ground and gave him a noogie until he laughed.

"Stop it!"

"Maybe that's what's in that tent," I said. "A big noogie!"

Brendan tried to hit me a few times, but missed.

"I'm just giving you some practice, so when it happens, you won't cry like Gabriel! You'll take it like a man!"

"Hunter!" he laughed. "Hunter, stop!"

He broke free. Then, he leapt onto my shoulders and tried to give me one. "No fair!" he called. "You're taller!"

"I've eaten all my vegetables. Spinach, straight from the can."

"So have I!"

"No way! If you had, you'd be just as tall as me."

"You're just growing faster, that's all."

"I am? That's funny because—"

Suddenly, I was interrupted by a steady, quiet beeping. I fell silent and began to listen. Brendan was still laughing. He had fallen off of my back and onto the ground. When I turned to face him, I saw him glancing down at his watch.

"What's that sound?"

"It's midnight," he told me. "We should go home."

"Midnight?"

And without really realizing what I was doing, I cast a glance over to the monkey bars.

"Midnight, huh? That's strange. I didn't realize it had gotten so late..."

My eyes traveled up and down the quiet street. Most of the houses were shrouded in darkness, all apart from one, where I could see light slanting into the front yard from the bay window—Harold's house.

"Let's go home," Brendan said again, getting to his feet. "Before we get into trouble..."

Suddenly, I recalled my dreams. I remembered the spiders scuttling out of the tent and those red eyes. I grabbed hold of Brendan's arm.

"Let's stay out a little later. I'm not tired. I'll just be lying in bed."

Brendan glanced down at his arm.

"Alright, just a little longer, I guess..."

I smiled and pulled Brendan into a headlock and gave him a noogie again. He laughed louder this time, and grabbed for my hair. When I finally let go, he stumbled to the ground and I saw something fall from his pocket.

"What's this?" I asked, grabbing hold of it.

"They're Gabriel's."

"Gabriel's?"

When I finally realized what they were, I frowned.

"Cigarettes?"

Brendan made a grab for them. "He asked me to hide them from Dad. Dad would be angry if he found out."

"Why? Does your dad actually believe all that stuff on the news about them? Mine says it's nonsense. 'There's nothing wrong with a good smoke,' he says."

Brendan shrugged. "I dunno, but ever since mine stopped using them, he hasn't been coughing as much. Mom just complains about his snoring now, which is a good thing."

I smiled. "I'm happy he's better. I was worried, you know."

"Yeah. Me too."

I turned the pack of cigarettes over in my hand. "But one can't hurt, right? Did you try any of them yet?"

He shook his head.

I put one in my mouth the same way I'd always seen the men do it on television. Afterward, I stuck out my pointer finger and pretended that my hand was a gun.

"Gimme all your money," I said, poking Brendan really hard in the chest with my make-believe pistol.

He laughed. "Who are you supposed to be?"

I pulled the cigarette from my mouth. "Those fat guys who wear the suits. You ever watch the pictures about the gangs and stuff? They play them on the higher channels, far away from all the kid stuff."

"No, I've never seen them."

I returned the cigarette to my mouth. Brendan tried to grab it away from me, but I didn't let him.

"C'mon, they're Gabriel's!"

"So what? He won't notice if a few are missing."

Brendan sighed. "Only one. Leave the rest."

I turned my hand into a gun again and jabbed it into the side of Brendan's head. "Who's gonna make me?"

Brendan tried to grab hold of me, but I laughed and leapt out of his reach. Then, I tackled him to the ground and we both laughed for a really long time until I fell silent because I heard something strange.

"Be quiet for a minute," I whispered. "What is that?"

Brendan couldn't hear it at first because he was still giggling. As the sound became louder, I realized that it was the chiming of an ice cream truck.

"Ice cream? This late?"

When I squinted through the darkness and onto the road, I saw the truck inching down the street. When the little bit of moonlight overhead broke through the clouds, it glistened across the side of the truck, and I saw rusty screws and water stains. There was even a large clown head welded to the top of the truck.

Then a clown voice, cackling above the chiming, echoed throughout the night. When my eyes narrowed and I squinted harder, I noticed a speaker protruding from the bowtie just beneath the clown's head.

"Boys and girls!" came the voice from inside. "Somebody on this street was a *naughty* boy!"

All down the street, house lights flickered on. I watched several people open their blinds and poke their heads out their bedroom windows.

"Brendan? Brendan, what is that?"

"I don't know…"

"C'mon. Let's get out of here..."

I began to turn away from the headlights of the truck, but Brendan stuck out an arm.

"It's stopping."

When I turned, I saw the ice cream truck had come to a halt before the house where the living room light had been cascading into the front yard. Now, I could see shapes and figures moving about through the window. I recognized Harold. He was shorter than the other silhouettes, rounder and with a fatter head.

"Boys and girls!" the voice called again. "Somebody on this street was a *naughty* boy!"

There was a terrible, high-pitched laugh. Brendan covered his ears and I grabbed hold of his hand without really meaning to.

"There's been a naughty boy! A naughty boy that didn't want to grow up!"

More lights flickered on until nearly every house had heads craning out of open windows. Now, above the ice cream truck speakers, I could hear shouting. It was coming from the moving shapes in the window of Harold's home. I recognized his mother's voice.

"*Harold... Harold*?!"

"How did they know?" I whispered, my eyes flashing over to the bush on the other side of the basketball court. "Was somebody watching that night? Did somebody... *see*?"

Several men, clothed in black, emerged from the truck. At first, I couldn't see their faces, but when I took several steps closer, I saw that they were wearing clown masks.

I heard Harold's mother again. "*Harold! Harold, you didn't?!*"

With their hands behind their backs, the men hurried up the front walkway. The chiming of the ice cream truck fell silent, and the clown voice whispered, "And now, he never will."

Ding dong! The doorbell.

Silence. The shapes in the window became still. The only thing that I could hear was the sound of crickets.

Ding dong!

No response.

Ding dong!
Ding dong!

The clown voice began to skip, like a scratched record. "Naughty… naughty… naughty…"

Then, finally, somebody opened the door. A small ray of light fell across the front porch, silhouetting the masked men. For several long moments, nobody moved. The faces in the doorway simply stared, and the masked men stared back. Then, all at once, there was screaming and shouting. I heard something shatter, probably a potted plant, and before I could even gasp, I saw Harold being led out of the house. He was red in the face and his shirt collar was wet with tears.

"Naughty… naughty… naughty…."

"No!" his mother called. She hurried out onto the front lawn, nearly tripping over her nightgown. "Please, don't!"

"Naughty… naughty… naughty…"

"Please!" she called again. "We didn't know! We'll take him to the town over! He'll see it! He'll see it, I swear!"

The chiming of the ice cream truck sounded again as the men led Harold to the back doors, which rattled open and released a fog of frigid air.

As I watched, I remembered Gabriel's voice. It echoed inside of my head and I couldn't get it out no matter how hard I tried. "Run away, if you can," it warned. "Far away, to a place where they can't find you or force you to close your eyes during the *green fireworks…*"

And before long, I heard the slamming of doors. The onlookers who had been watching from their windows returned to bed and darkness fell once more. As the truck crawled down the street and out of sight, the only sound that could be heard above the distant chiming was the sound of Harold's sobbing mother. She was on her knees, screaming something that I couldn't understand.

Even years later, nobody in the neighborhood ever found out what really happened to Harold Stacy. All that anyone knows is that they took him away from us that night and nobody ever saw him again. Some of the older boys say that they cut him open and used his blood to make red paint. Others said that they ground up his bones to make popsicle sticks.

All that I know is that I miss waving to him on my bike ride to Brendan's.

The Night I Saw A Clown Inside My Kitchen

Lucky number 13. Nearly two years after Harold Stacy disappeared into the back of that truck, I was blowing out the candles of my thirteenth birthday cake at a crusty table in the corner of the local bowling alley. My parents bought me a red bicycle that year. I knew they spent extra money on it because they wanted to make me happy before "it" happened.

I went riding a few days later even though it was mid-November and the air hurt when I breathed it in. I fell once and cried for a really long time. It didn't hurt when I fell. I don't know why I cried. I think I just needed to.

That year, when summer came around again and the cold air grew hot, the Barnaby commercials on television were more frequent than I ever remember them being. One night in late June, Barnaby's sponsored the broadcast of one of my favorite cartoons. After the program ended, a clown came onto the television to talk about childhood.

My house was pretty quiet that night, or at least, the downstairs was. The microwave was humming, but the tray wasn't spinning because it was too old and needed fixing. I was cooking one of those frozen dinners, nothing special, just the kind that came in the red boxes and were only ninety nine cents.

Despite being two years older, I didn't feel any different. I still loved the same things and dreamt the same dreams. Even though I felt the same, I noticed changes all around me. Mom and Dad kept telling me that I was too old to be watching cartoons. Dad let my brother watch them because he was only ten at the time, but never me. He'd change the channel if he saw me.

But that night, Dad wasn't home and my mom was upstairs with Mr. Roberts. She was always really loud when she was with him, but I guess they both liked it that way. I could tell that he did things to her that my dad didn't do, although I didn't want to, and it was easier to ignore the moaning when cartoons were on.

I stirred my watery mashed potatoes until they looked so thick and gray that they could've been wet cement.

"*Can you imagine?*" a voice whispered from the television, "*A world without any adults? A world filled with kids?*"

I crossed over to the refrigerator and grabbed a carton of milk from inside. I said hello to Susan Smith, the missing girl on the back who was smiling up at me. After taking a big swig, I spit it all out into the sink.

It was old milk. The girl on the back was found dead, anyway. They found her all cut up inside a bunch of rolled-up tarp. Her body was somewhere behind the A&P, in one of those black, rubber drains. I guess that's how you can tell that you need new milk— when the girl on the back's been dead a week already.

As I dumped the milk into the sink, the words, "BARNABY'S TRAVELING CARNIVAL" slithered across the television screen behind me.

A clown stepped into frame— the one whose voice I'd heard. He was wearing too much makeup. The red paint was fading around his lips and running onto his teeth. Behind him, a chorus of children were clapping and laughing. The clown giggled along with them.

"It's that time of year, kiddos!" he shouted. "We'd just like to remind all of our beautiful kiddos out there whose thirteenth birthdays falls between July 17th of last year and July 10th of this year… childhood ends in two weeks."

After an awkward transition, the television showed a man clothed in a tight, radiating outfit walking across a tightrope. Beneath him, a lioness growled and swatted at him with her paws. The man let out a terrible scream as he fell and the words "2 WEEKS UNTIL CHILDHOOD ENDS," appeared across the screen.

Behind me, I heard the hum of my garage door, followed by a light crash. My Dad was home, probably pulling into the garage with half-open eyes and knocking over my brother's crate of balls and baseball mittens.

There was a shout from upstairs, belonging to my mother, and suddenly, the floorboards were creaking instead of the bed frames.

"What... what time is it?! Get! Get out!"

Mr. Robert's voice followed. It was normally so composed, but not tonight. "Oh... *oh!*"

The clown began to speak again, and as he did, Mr. Roberts came skidding into the kitchen with a hand on his undone belt. I didn't remove my eyes from the floor as I heard the back door slam. Normally, he smiled at me before he went, apologetically, like that could make it better.

On the television screen, the clown's smile had faded. "Because can you imagine a world where nobody ever grew up? Kiddos, I'm going to tell you something. I was very sick once. So sick, that I couldn't play or have any fun with the other boys."

He leaned forward, so far that he was nearly spilling out into my kitchen.

"But my mom made me all better! She took my temperature with one of those sticks that they put under your tongue and she called for the doctor to come see me. But who would've made me better if the world was filled with kids? I'd have only gotten sicker, because everybody would've been too busy skipping rope outside and swinging on the swings."

The clown finally drew back, further into the frame, and I felt like I could breathe again. He extended his arms, gave a quick twirl, and then let out a cackle that made the hairs on my arms rise.

"But cheer up! No frowns! Because the fireworks will light up the sky every night! Red and green ones… of celebration! To thank you for ending your childhood and keeping this world a beautiful place!"

I heard the front door open. I saw my dad's shadow sliding down the walls as he trudged his way inside. The sound of exploding fireworks sounded from the television while the clown continued to twirl.

I watched his tongue slide across the chipping paint on his lips before he bowed. "Don't dawdle! When you see red in the sky, you know what time it is! Turn those cute, little faces of yours to the sky! Come on down!"

The Night Before My Childhood Ended

They closed off some of the back roads when the carnival arrived. If I looked hard enough from my bedroom window, I could see the trucks and tents being set up in a lot beside the lake that I used to swim in when I was young.

I had an argument with my Dad one night because I didn't want to go inside that tent, but no matter what I said, he shook his head and spat, "Do you know what they'd do to you, to *us*?"

When he said that, my mind returned to Harold. I remembered that truck and that awful clown laugh, but I didn't understand. I heard it all the time: *they*, but I never quite knew who *they* were. *They* stamp your hand when you come out of the Freak Tent and write your name down in a big, tattered book. When the carnival is gone, somebody, probably a lady with thick glasses that make her look like a bug, pages through all the names and makes sure every 13-year-old in town went inside that tent. She's one of *them*.

The stamp is a firework. A big, red firework.

Brendan decided to go inside that tent with me so we could end our childhoods together. We met at the playground by our house the night before the third day of Barnaby's. We sat on the slide with all the black scuffs on it. A cold front had settled that week, and we needed to wear jackets despite it being mid-summer.

Although we couldn't see the carnival, we could hear it. Every few moments, loud chatter and applause erupted from somewhere in the distance.

"Do you think we'll be okay?" Brendan asked me.

"Don't worry about that. Not today. It's your birthday. Say, I have something for you."

His eyes grew wide when I pulled out a card that I had drawn for him. It was taped atop a box which I had wrapped with shimmering, red paper— the only kind that I could find in the basement.

I pushed it into his hand. "Happy Birthday."

He laughed. It was nice to see him smile, because I hadn't seen it that entire night and something about it made me feel really warm and lost somewhere inside myself.

"You got me a present?"

"Yeah, but don't shake it! You'll smear the icing more than it already is."

His smile broadened. "It's cake?"

"Read the card first!"

He did. He read it aloud and then opened the small box and we ate the cake together and I sang "Happy Birthday" to him in a really nasally voice that made him laugh. Then, I pulled his ear thirteen times like our teachers used to do in the second grade and he wasn't nervous about the carnival anymore.

* * * * *

That night after Brendan went back home, I sat on my bed and stared out the window. A mile or so away, the carnival lights danced and beckoned me forward like the rays of a lighthouse.

I didn't sleep well that night. I kept dreaming about rusty cages filled with death and disease, or some horrible secret that I hadn't known existed before.

The sun didn't really rise the following morning. The sky was a gray color and the weatherman called for rain that entire evening. At dinner, I asked my father if the carnival would be cancelled. He laughed and then said with a mouthful of pork roast, "They wouldn't close that damn fair if missiles were falling from the sky, let alone a few raindrops."

My mom stood up from the table a few moments later. "My baby..." she whispered, stroking my cheek and staring into my eyes. "Tonight's the night? You've decided?"

I nodded, but didn't say anything.

She pulled me into a long hug and all that I wanted to do was squirm my way out of it because the television behind her was lit with a Barnaby's ad that said, "WILL YOUR CHILDHOOD END TONIGHT?"

I met Brendan in his backyard before we left for the carnival. Together, we laid down in the grass and stared up at the sky because we both felt like we should watch clouds one last time before we went.

"I wish there was some blue in the sky," I said to him, and he just nodded.

* * * * *

The parking lot outside of the carnival was filled with red Chevy cars. I gave 50 cents to an old woman inside the wooden booth labeled, "BARNABY'S ADMISSION TICKETS." Brendan dug through his pockets beside me. When he removed his trembling hands, several nickels fell to the grass, so I handed the woman another two quarters and said to Brendan, "Don't worry, Mom gave me money. She didn't want me to say anything to my dad about... you know."

The woman took the coins and handed me two tickets. I forced a polite smile and headed through the gate into the carnival. Inside, children were giggling and weaving through the crowds. They all had red balloons tied around their wrists. Beside them, their fathers jostled change in their pockets and their mothers fanned themselves with carnival flyers.

A man with a bowler hat shouted to the passing crowd from atop a barrel. "Come on down! The elephant slaughtering will be startin' in no more than 20 minutes, folks! You heard me right! 20 minutes! Check those watches of yours! Right this way, right this way!"

When I tried to catch Brendan's gaze, to make him feel better about it all, he wouldn't look up from the dirt path beneath us.

"I just want to let you know," I told him, "even though our childhood is ending tonight, I promise I'll always be one around you."

He smiled and we twisted our pinkies around one another's. As I was staring into his eyes, they seemed to grab hold of mine and I felt an urge to pull him closer, but I heard an awful cackle and we both turned to see the black outline of the Freak Tent further down the path.

"Should we do it now?" I asked, trying to make my voice sound more sturdy than it was. "Do you think we should just get it over with?"

Brendan bit his bottom lip, which I noticed was red and swollen because he'd been chewing on it all night. "They say we won't sleep for a while after we go inside…"

"I know they say that," I said, forcing a weak smile, "but I'll be right here beside you."

As I squeezed his hand, I heard a new voice. It echoed above the cheerful, carefree musings of the fairgoers. "Step right up!" it cried. "See the Freak Tent! All 13-year-olds and older! Step right up!"

And suddenly, I remembered Gabriel and his bloodied hands. The pathetic smile that I'd been hiding behind unfurled and my eyes fixated themselves on the Freak Tent opening that was swallowing up happy guests and spitting out kids that looked like they had a stomach ache.

"Maybe we won't sleep for awhile," I whispered, "but that doesn't scare me. A couple bad dreams don't scare me."

Brendan looked up. "You're not afraid?"

I shook my head. "They're just dreams, aren't they? Besides, Dad tells me dreams are silly. I stopped dreaming them a long time ago."

49

The Night The World Was Ruined

I thought about Harold Stacy as Brendan and I waited in the line that wrapped around the Freak Tent. I wondered what he must have felt, sitting alone in his room and watching the fireworks on the final night of Barnaby's. He probably chewed down his fingernails until they bled because he hadn't ended his childhood and knew something bad was going to happen.

I considered skipping the carnival, too. A few weeks back, I packed a suitcase. I planned to run away just like the gangsters do in the movies when they know the cops are after them. I didn't even make it to the end of my yard before I cried and hurried back inside because I thought about Brendan and how I'd never get to see him again. While we waited in line that night, I could see a heartbeat in those hazel eyes of his, and although they reflected the neon lights of the carnival so beautifully, there was a fear inside them, deep down.

The wooden sign above us, warped from too much rain, swung forebodingly overtop of our heads. It read, "FREAK TENT," and I could tell that Brendan was trying his hardest not to look at it.

There were clowns walking up and down the line, smiling and tying balloon animals for all of the 13-year-olds. "Thank you!" they'd cackle while thrusting elephant-shaped balloons in everyone's hands, "for ending your childhood tonight!"

It wasn't long before we were next in line, just inches from the entrance that separated us from whatever secrets and monsters that our world kept hidden in the dark.

We paid a quarter to the man at the booth and he drew back the curtains, just enough so that we could slip inside the tent. His fingers were long. He had greasy hair and a crooked nose. The curtain was velvet— I remember that clearly and I'm not sure why.

"And when you two come out," he whispered as we stepped into the darkness, "don't look in the funhouse mirrors for awhile. You'll see something in your eyes... something that wasn't there before."

And then he laughed and the curtain swung closed behind us.

"Are you ready?" I asked Brendan, although I couldn't see him, and I grabbed hold of his hand and squeezed it because I knew it'd make him feel better.

The lighting was dim in there, there was a lot of smoke, too, and before my eyes could adjust, I whispered to Brendan, "It smells funny, kind of like... that kennel down the road from your house. Remember that? Huh? You remember?"

I couldn't hear his answer, because suddenly, there was laughter. It sounded high and sharp. When the black haze began to dissolve into shapes, I saw bands of people rattling cans against silver bars. The burning tips of their cigarettes speckled the darkness like candlelight.

Brendan cried out in fear. His foot got caught on something that neither of us could see, and he fell to the floor.

"I... I'm bleeding!" he yelped. His voice cracked, but I couldn't see his cheeks redden in the darkness like they always did when that happened. "What *is* this place?"

* * * * *

I asked my father that same question a few nights before. The television was whispering jazz in the corner of my kitchen. My mother was humming loudly to herself and drifting in and out of the kitchen with a glass of wine.

"You step inside a boy and leave a man!" my father said, slamming his fist onto the table and rattling the plates. "Isn't that what you want to be, Hunter? Don't you want to be like your *father*?"

I nodded fervently. My eyes were wide, probably fixated on whatever was dangling from his beard.

The cat screeched and leapt out of the room when my Father hit the table again. "You're soft, you hear? You're turning soft!"

I thought about that, too, when I'd been standing in the line for the Freak Tent. Was I turning soft? Even if I was, would my father still be proud of me? As I daydreamed about a future where things were okay and my father still loved me, I saw a group of thirteen-year-olds stumble through the Freak Tent curtain, back into the moonlit carnival, and hurry over to a small table while sobbing over bloodied hands. Behind the table, a woman was perched on a stool. She looked like a hungry vulture and gazed at the children through glasses that seemed to magnify her eyes to twice their size.

"It's a quarter to get inside," the booth operator said to me with a smile, and I pulled my gaze away from the gaunt woman and crying kids. He smiled at me and hit his cane against a small sign that read, "FREAK TENT - 25 CENTS."

"I'm paying for me and my friend," I said, dropping two quarters into the glass jar beside the sign.

The man leaned forward. "Say… how old are you, boy?"

"Thirteen…" I mumbled. "Just turned this past November."

"And your friend?"

"The same. He just turned yesterday."

The man nodded. He handed Brendan and I both a chunk of cement block that had deep, red stains. It was wet, so I couldn't get a grip on it at first.

"Are you ready?" he asked us. "For the end of childhood?"

When we asked what to do with the red block, he just smiled and pulled off his hat to slick back his oily hair before turning to Brendan. *"Happy Birthday."*

* * * * *

"I... I'm bleeding!" Brendan said again, still holding onto his knee.

"It's okay. It'll all be okay because—"

My voice fell silent when somebody shrieked with laughter. I felt something brush against my shoulder, and I turned to see a clown skipping through the darkness while honking a large, golden horn. He grabbed hold of my arm and pulled me through the crowd. Brendan shouted and I grabbed hold of him, too. Together, we stumbled through the crowd and across a large clearing where several men were twirling women to jazz music.

The clown finally came to a halt at the front of the crowd. He turned to face Brendan and me, placed a hand over of our eyes, and whispered for us to close them.

"When you open them again, you'll understand," he told us, his breath smelling like stale cigarette smoke. "For a quarter a year, you can be God, even if it's just for a moment."

I felt him remove his hands from over my eyes, but I still kept them tightly closed. When he honked his horn in my face, I took a step back and nearly tripped over Brendan.

And then, I opened my eyes.

Everything swam into focus.

I saw it. Everything. All it once.

It hit me, taking my breath with it. My heart seemed to disappear, because I couldn't feel it anymore, so I gripped my chest with my hand to try and make sure it was still there.

And in that very second— I grew up. I forgot all about swinging on the swings at the playground and being young.

I grew up the moment I saw the eyes of the boys and girls of the Freak Tent.

53

The laughter around us chorused louder. I spun around until I was so close to Brendan that we were nearly kissing. I was suddenly out of breath. Something hurt inside my chest and I felt my heartbeat again.

"Why are there...?"

"My brother says..."

"They must've done something terrible! Like kill or steal! Brendan, that's what this is all about! They're trying to scare us! They want us to be good!"

"Hunter..."

"The people in those cages... they must've done something! That's the only thing that makes sense!"

But even as I said it, I had a terrible feeling in my gut that what I was saying wasn't true. When I turned around again to face the bars, the first thing that I saw was a boy lying on the ground and bleeding from the temple. His eyes were open, so I didn't know if he was alive or dead. There were flies crawling up and down his arms, which were covered in dirt and scabs. Beside him, a naked girl was watching a clown on the other side of the bars pulling a large stream of ribbons from his mouth.

"FREAKS!" somebody shouted. He stuck his cigarette through the gap between the bars and pressed the tip to the girl's arm. She leapt backward. My heart leapt, too.

"Right, Brendan? These are bad people in these cages, right?"

Somebody laughed across the tent, just like all the others, except this time, I recognized the voice.

I saw Michael Evans— the boy who wore the clown mask the night the older boys dared us to go to the playground after dark. He was tossing pennies at a boy in one of the cages. Michael had on his letterman jacket like he always did, and he was surrounded with a few burly jocks and girls with powdered faces.

"Michael... Michael's here too?"

"Hey!" he shouted to the boy through the bars. "I'm talking to you! You're not deaf, too, are ya?"

The pennies bounced off the boy's back and pattered to the ground. The sign above the cage read, "BLIND BOY. WATCH HIM ALL DAY! MAKE FACES! YOU CAN SEE HIM, BUT HE CAN'T SEE YOU!"

"Hey!" Michael continued. "What do you say, huh? Would you suck my dick for a nickel? I'll show you where it is!"

My eyes traveled further down the line of cages, until they fell still on a cage surrounded with several housewives. Inside, a girl was crouched several feet away from the bars. She had chubby fingers and belly fat that spilled overtop her naked thighs. The sign above the cage read, "PIG. TOSS HER SCRAPS! SHE'S STARVING FOR YOUR ATTENTION!"

The housewives surrounding the cage pointed and scoffed. I recognized one of them— Mrs. Roberts. A pearl necklace was draped around her long, thin neck.

It was strange. She gave me leftover cookies one day and talked about books at our house. Did she go inside the Freak Tent a lot, too?

I examined more signs. I saw "DYKE" and "TRANNY."

Then, I saw Pastor Moore. He was standing two cages down, looking at a young girl, probably no older than two. I couldn't read the sign above her because it was too worn, but she had sunken eyes with an upward slant to them.

Brendan tugged on the sleeve of my shirt.

"Hunter," he whispered. "Hunter, we need to—"

I turned to see what he was pointing at.

"We need to get our thumbs—"

There was a shout. Michael Evans had grabbed hold of one of the caged boy's arms through the bars and began to smack at it with his chunk of cement block. When Michael finally stopped, he pressed his thumb against the boy's bleeding forearm until his thumb was coated with blood. His friends did the same.

"No," I whispered, turning to face Brendan. "I… I don't think I can…."

I let the piece of cement fall from my hand, where it hit the grass floor with a thud.

Then, the tears came. "I understand it now… I understand why everybody paints their lawn red and dresses the same and acts the same…"

Brendan squeezed my hand, although I was suddenly afraid that somebody would see.

"I have an idea," he whispered.

As more and more people continued to scream inside the Freak Tent, and I heard the sickening bang of cement being hit against bars and bones, Brendan wiped my thumb across the scrape on his knee and I felt my finger wet with blood. Then, he did the same to his own.

"C'mon," he said, leading me forward.

"Yeah," I breathed. "Come on…"

We began to head for the exit, and as we did, we were interrupted by Mr. Roberts, who was wearing a suit and slipping inside the tent through the curtain. I nearly collided with him.

"Hunter!" he chuckled awkwardly. He clapped me on the shoulder. "I'm looking for my wife, of course…"

"I was just leaving…"

He gave me a curious look. "This is your first time in here, isn't it?"

I didn't answer him, but his eyes traveled to my bloody thumb and he knew. He bent down slightly, until he was eye level with me and I couldn't look away easily, although I tried.

"First time, huh? I remember when I turned thirteen. It gets easier. And look on the bright side…"

He gently twisted my chin to face him, until we were staring into one another's eyes.

"Everything is going to change now, isn't it?"

And he returned to full height, gave me one last pat on the back, and headed toward his wife, who was still gossiping with other women in the corner and twirling her pearl necklace.

Brendan pulled at my sleeve again and we continued out of the tent.

"Quickly," he said, "Before it dries…"

As we were leaving, I noticed cursive lettering across the plastic tarp of the tent that hung over top of the exit. In faded letters, it read, "How terrible it would be to be a green light in a sea of red."

The Night My Hand Was Stamped And I Was One Of Them

"What did you two think, eh?" the booth operator said with a twisted smile. His breath smelled of brandy, like my Mom's. He grabbed hold of my hand and pressed down on the back of it with a rubber stamp. "Tell me, are you afraid?"

"No," I lied. "I'm not afraid."

He nodded and released my hand. "Watch the fireworks tonight— but only the red ones. Only those. They watch. Be careful."

"Our parents are waiting up for us at home. It's late."

His toothy grin didn't fade. He bowed. "Make sure you get your names down in that book over there."

He gestured behind us, where the woman who looked like a vulture was seated at the small table. She didn't smile— only ushered us forward.

"Quickly, quickly. Name please. Last, then first."

While I mumbled my name, she wrote it out in thick, red ink inside her stale book. Then, she pressed my thumb down beside my name. At first, when she pulled my hand up, the paper stuck to my skin because of the stickiness of the blood. The page finally broke away from my finger and Brendan did the same. Once we were done and our fingerprints were inside that book, Brendan gave me a dark look and we hurried away from the bloody book and past a group of clowns that were smearing pies across each other's faces.

* * * * *

The carnival paths were less crowded than they were when we had first come. In the distance, I could hear the distressed trumpeting of several elephants, followed by loud cheering.

Brendan and I collapsed onto a bench outside of a greasy looking truck that served turkey legs. The vendor of the stand was flirting with a girl on the other side of the truck. The backs of several other food tends served as walls that shielded us from the crowded pathways on all four sides.

I looked down at the blood on Brendan's knee from when he had stumbled in the tent. He was scraped up pretty badly and I knew he was hurting because he squeezed his nails so hard into the area surrounding his knee that small, red indents outlined the wound like dotted lines on a map.

"You okay?" I asked, kneeling before him.

"Who started this, huh? Who started Barnaby's Carnival?"

I pulled a wad of napkins from a metal container on the table. I dabbed his knee.

"I don't know."

"Do you think," he began, "that they'd put people like us in there? If they found out what we did… what we *do*?"

I swallowed hard. "Nobody has to know what we do up there."

"I'm just scared, that's all. My brother saw somebody like me, once, and he smiled so… so *wickedly*."

I wiped the last bit of blood cleanly from his knee. Then, I leaned forward and kissed it, smiled, and looked up.

"There, all better."

And when I'd finished, he gave me a long, hard look, one that I recognized. He had only given it to me twice before. The first was the night he had fallen on the playground.

The second was the year we turned twelve. We were both sitting together on the top of the Ferris Wheel. You know that moment? The moment when it it stops to let somebody on and you're just hanging there, so high up in the sky and nobody, not a *soul* in the world, can touch you up there?

Brendan gave me a look up there, last year, and we kissed for a long time because I always had a feeling that we should.

The Night We Tied Flowers Around The Monkey Bars

The red stamp on the back of my hand itched like poison ivy. I scratched at it my entire way home, until the skin felt raw. I didn't speak to Brendan while I walked, although I listened to his breathing, which was just as quick and shallow as mine.

A few times, I cast a glance over my shoulder at the carnival. I could still see the Ferris Wheel just above the treeline. The top gondola was rocking back and forth.

Suddenly, I felt very cold and I wished it were last summer again. I missed how Brendan's lips tasted sweet and we were both nervous, but something about kissing him made my stomach feel like it was inside out.

Children were still at the playground when we finally arrived in our neighborhood again. They laughed and caught fireflies. A few of them were racing their bicycles up and down the street.

"Hey!" one of them shouted to us. "My brother got his ball stuck in a tree! You're tall, can you get it down?"

I didn't respond at first because I was still trying really hard to remember the scent of Brendan's hair instead of the stench of the Freak Tent.

"Hey!" he said, this time louder. "We can't get it down ourselves!"

"Hunter," I heard Brendan say, and I finally looked up, because when Brendan said my name, it sounded a lot like music.

"What did you say?"

"Our ball!" the boy said again, impatiently. "It's stuck in the tree over there!"

He pointed and my eyes flashed to a tree just beside the playground. I remembered how the older boys had tossed our ball into the bushes several years ago and it had taken us forever to get out because our arms weren't long enough.

"If you stand on tiptoe, you'll reach it!" he told us.

I followed him to the tree. He jumped once to try to get it, but he was still nearly a foot too short. When I outstretched my hand to knock it down, the little boy gasped.

"Is that...?"

The ball came tumbling down. "There. Don't throw it up into the trees anymore, or it'll get stuck again and you'll have to get it down yourself."

"Wow!" he beamed, ignoring what I had just said. "Is this your first night being a grown up? I'm counting down the days until my childhood gets to end..."

I looked down at the red stamp on the back of my hand. There were nail marks and scratches all across the back of my hand because it had itched so badly.

"I'm only eight this year," the boy continued. "But they say I'll be thirteen before I know it."

"Is that so?"

"Of course! Hey... where are you going?"

I had begun walking across the playground. The little boy waddled after me.

"We should get home," I heard Brendan say, but I didn't answer him because I didn't want him to leave.

"Are you going to play on the playground?" the little boy asked me. "Can you still do that?"

"Of course I can."

"You're so much taller than me. You're probably tall enough to reach the monkey bars. I can't yet, but Mom says I'll be able to soon. Hopefully I'll get that tall before my childhood ends."

My eyes traveled from the boy's bright eyes to the monkey bars, which were empty because all of the other children were either swinging on the swings or climbing on the fort.

Then, all at once and without any warning, thunder exploded above. In the distance, just above the tree lining, we saw a few flashes of lightning in the sky. The little boy gasped, and so did all the others. With his ball cradled to his chest, he gave us one final look before shouting, "Thanks!" and heading off for home as the first rain drops began to fall.

I didn't move at all, even when I felt my bangs become damp from the rain.

"Hunter," Brendan whispered, wiping a few droplets of rain from my face, "are you going to be okay?"

The rain fell harder. For a few moments, I was distracted by the red paint bleeding off of all of the leaves and bushes. It ran down the sidewalks and into the streets before disappearing down the sewer drains.

"I'll be okay." I finally said, pulling my eyes away. "Will *you*?"

Another crackle of thunder exploded above, so I couldn't hear what Brendan said, but I didn't need to, because something caught my eye and I don't think I would've been able to listen to him anyway.

"Do you see those? Just across the playground?"

Brendan turned to where I was pointing. He wiped the rain from his eyes and squinted through the darkness toward the dozen white roses that were dancing in the wind.

"They must have just bloomed," he said. "The truck will be by tomorrow to paint them red."

I bit my lip. "Let's pick them before they do."

"Why do you want to...?"

"Come on!"

Brendan tried to protest, but I had already grabbed hold of his hand and began pulling him across the playground.

"Hunter, stop. We need to go home. Our parents..."

"They say we've grown up. They say we aren't children anymore…"

"So?"

"So they can't tell us what to do, okay? They can't be worried about us."

I stopped just before the large bush. I pulled one of the flowers from the branches and brought it close to my eyes.

"Have you ever seen something so… odd?"

Brendan didn't answer. Instead, he watched me pull more flowers from the bush and push the stems into the pockets of my pants.

"Are you going to keep them?" he asked.

I was just about to respond, but lightning flashed across the sky and the blinding light reflected off of the metal of the monkey bars.

"I think I have a better idea…"

Brendan followed my gaze to the dripping bars. "A better one?"

I started picking more roses and pushing them into Brendan's hands.

"What are you doing?"

"He never had a funeral, did he? They just took him away and nobody ever talks about him or remembers him anymore."

"We remember him."

"But nobody knows where they buried him, and I'm sure nobody puts flowers on his grave. I really don't like that, Brendan. I don't like that at all."

Brendan didn't argue or say anything else. He just nodded and made sure nobody was looking out their windows.

And nobody was.

So, in the downpour that night, Brendan and I tied a bunch of white roses around the third monkey bar from the left-- the one that Tommy Swanson had died beneath. We made sure that none of the red metal could be seen anymore. Then, we sat down and stared up at the sky and pretended that we could see stars. And even though we couldn't, it was very special.

After a few hours, Brendan finally went home, and I was nervous for him to go because it meant that I would be alone. The rain had finally stopped and the entire playground was damp. Soon after, the moon appeared from behind the rain clouds and I could see a few stars if I squinted hard enough.

I continued to sit on the wet mulch of the playground with wet eyes, staring up at the sky until I fell asleep without really meaning to.

* * * * *

I didn't have any nightmares even though I was afraid that I would never have happy dreams again. Instead, I dreamt about Brendan's lips because I had stared at them while he was lying beside me on the playground.

I also dreamt about something wonderful and strange. It was dark inside my dreams, full of storm clouds and lightning. I couldn't see anything at all, but I could hear breathing. I wasn't frightened, because the breathing sounded like it belonged to an old friend.

When my dream finally become clear, I saw a boy staring back at me. He was hard to recognize at first because he had changed so much since I last saw him. His body had filled out and his arms were bigger. I wouldn't have recognized him if I hadn't seen the rope burns around his neck.

"Is that...? Are you....?"

I reached out a hand and touched his bare chest. He wasn't wearing a shirt and I recognized his shoulders because they were scarred from acne. His hair was longer than I remembered, and it was pushed back like the boys in the pictures that they show down at the old movie theater across town. His lips were pretty and full, just like Brendan's, but a cigarette was tucked between his and he seemed to be chewing on it instead of smoking it.

"Tommy....?" I breathed, squinting through the darkness.

He leapt back as soon as my fingertips reached his abdomen. His pale, translucent body flickered like a dying movie projection.

"Tommy?" I said, struggling to sit up. "Is it really you?"

"Who are you?" he demanded, eyes wide. The cigarette slipped from his lips and landed on the ground at my feet. "How do you know my name?"

His eyes flashed over to the monkey bars, which dissolved from the darkness, and he must've seen the white flowers that Brendan and I tied around the third bar from the left because he let out a gasp and ran a finger across the delicate, white petals.

"Did you put these here?"

There was a sudden beeping that echoed throughout the canvas of the dream world, and I wasn't sure where it came from.

"What's that sound?" I groaned, covering my ears because it seemed to be louder than anything I'd ever heard.

"Did you put these here?" he demanded again.

When my eyes caught sight of his wrists, I saw the gleaming surface of a watch. Both of the hands were on the twelve.

"Hey!" he bellowed. "Did you put these here?"

I nodded, but didn't remove my hands from my ears. "My friend helped me. His name's Brendan…"

Tommy pulled one of the roses from the bar and brought it to his nose. When he turned to face me, instead of his eyes brightening, the veins around his pupils seemed to fill with blood and pulsate.

"What do you know about any of this?! Huh?"

"I… I thought…"

He began pulling more flowers from the bar. The petals twirled to the mulch, where they seemed to curl up and disappear.

66

"I don't want these here!" he cried. "Take them down! Get out of here!"

"I'm sorry... Tommy, don't..."

He ripped the last flower from the bar and tossed it to the ground. "Why the hell would you do that?"

His watch continued to beep, and he stared at me, silently. His eyes filled up with tears.

"Christ, kid," he whispered. "Why would you do something like that?"

And suddenly, as he faded away, darkness crept up on me and I woke up, wide-eyed, in my reality.

* * * * *

The Wizard of Oz was playing on the television in the kitchen when I returned home. Dorothy and her friends were skipping down the yellow brick road. My Father was asleep, face down on the kitchen table. When I closed the back door, he stirred slightly and opened his eyes.

"Why aren't you in bed?" I asked, getting myself a glass of water from the kitchen sink because I was anxious and didn't know what else to do with my hands.

He didn't answer. Instead, he grabbed hold of my arm and examined the bleeding outline of the red firework on the back of my hand.

His eyes grew wide. "Tell me, were you afraid?"

"No, I was not afraid."

"Not at all? What did you see when you looked into their eyes?"

I pulled my hand away. "I didn't look into their eyes."

"Not at all? Not even when—"

"Dad..."

"If you had, you would've seen—"

67

I interrupted him. "Dad, I know what I would've seen."

Silence followed, apart from Dorothy's laughter, which filled the room like a beautiful perfume. When my eyes flickered over to the television again, I almost choked on my water. On the screen, there were large, glittering buildings made of *green* and when Dorothy spoke, I could've sworn she said *Emerald City.*

"Somebody's going to lose their job over that," my father muttered, watching the television, too. "Playing the old version. I thought they trashed all of those reels."

"There's an... *old* version?"

As I watched the flickering screen, I fell in love with the green towers. My eyes grew wide because I'd always seen Dorothy skipping to *Ruby* City, which never sounded quite right and never really matched anybody's lips when spoken. I never realized that a time existed when people didn't edit out the green in the movies.

My father turned to face me again, and when he did, a smile broke across his face. "I'm proud of you, son. When I went in there for the first time, do you know what I did?"

I shook my head.

He chuckled. "I got sick. All down my front. But then I learned. Hunter, there are always going to be people in cages, somewhere. And if it's not them, it's you."

"What if we just stop putting people in cages? Then what?"

He shook his head. "They put themselves in there. Every single one of them had a choice, and they chose wrong. You're young, but you'll understand soon."

I didn't respond. He took my silence as acceptance.

"Being just like everybody else is *easy*," he continued. "It's the easiest thing you'll ever do. You'll never have to leave. You'll never have to worry. You'll never need to go searching for something, because when people go searching for themselves, they always get lost because there's *nothing* to find."

I didn't believe him. Instead, I watched the television screen because the Emerald City was glittering and it made me feel happy to know that Dorothy found something beautiful just by skipping down a road with other people who were just as lost as her.

My dad gave me one final smile and squeezed my shoulder. "Turn off the television before you go to bed."

And with that, he left me standing alone in the kitchen. The Wizard of Oz faded to darkness and the commercials began to roll. I heard the familiar, high-pitched voice of the clown from Barnaby's.

"It's that time of year, kiddos!"

The glass nearly slipped from my hand. The chorus of children clapped and screamed.

"Hold your applause boys and girls! You'll be needing it for the shows you're about to see! Trapeze artists—"

Within seconds, I jabbed the power button and the television went black. From there, I hurried over to the sink, cried out, and tried to scrub the back of my hand until the red firework was gone.

The Year Before Brendan's Father Died

Mr. Roberts was right when he told me that everything was going to change. In late July, less than two months after the carnival closed its gates and traveled one town over, my little brother had his eleventh birthday party. Half of my family was there, including my aunt and uncle who announced their split two years prior but never carried through with it. A few of my brother's friends were there, too, with little red party hats atop their oddly shaped heads.

We were all sitting outside under the beating sun at a few picnic tables that gave us splinters if we touched them wrong. My mother drifted through the screen door and into the backyard with a large cake decorated with dripping candles. Atop it, in cursive icing, "HAPPY 11th BIRTHDAY, JAMIE" was written.

"It's everyone's favorite. *Red* velvet!"

Everyone leaned in to watch Jamie blow out the candles. My mother pulled out her Kodak camera and laughed while snapping photographs.

"Almost, honey! Just two more candles!"

Jamie finally blew out all the candles and thin ghosts of smoke drifted skyward. Everyone cheered and clapped. Soon after, he began opening presents. He left the largest one for last.

"A big box!" he exclaimed, raising it into the air. "This one is so big!"

"Honey, tell us who it's from!"

He examined the tag. "It's from Joshua!"

The crowd nodded and a small boy to his left smiled broadly.

He began tearing off the paper and several strands blew across the yard in the mid-summer breeze.

"It's a… it's a…"

Toy car. A red one. Jamie laughed and my mother squealed. She turned to the picnic table full of adult relatives and exclaimed, "Oh, another one!"

I smiled because everyone else was. My aunt, who was sitting beside me, leaned in closely. "What a lovely gift," she whispered. "You got him the same one, didn't you?"

I nodded and she patted my leg while her lips broke into a smile, almost like she was eating something too sweet. I looked away, uncomfortable, toward the empty seat beside me.

I wished Brendan were there. I'd invited him to come, but he couldn't make it because his Dad started coughing really badly that summer and nobody could figure out what was wrong with him. One night, Brendan even said he saw his dad standing in the bathroom and bleeding all over his hands. The door wasn't closed all the way, and Brendan didn't want to watch, but he couldn't stop himself.

He said that the entire front of the mirror was covered with blood droplets. The blood was coming out of his father's nose and everything.

That was the night that Brendan yelled at Gabriel for the first time in years. While Brendan stood outside of the bathroom door and watched his father spraying blood all over the mirror like he sprayed red paint all over the grass, Gabriel crept out of his room. He and Brendan just stared at each other until Brendan finally shouted, "I can't get any sleep in this house, anymore! Because you're up all night, hitting those damn bed posts and he's up all night *coughing* and I just can't take it! I just want to sleep! You hear me?!"

As Brendan stormed down the hall toward Gabriel, he stopped when he saw that Gabriel was crying. That made Brendan cry, too. He pulled Gabriel into a hug and it was the first time they'd done that since they were little boys.

"Gabriel," he choked out through his tears, "he's *dying*, isn't he?"

* * * * *

Sometimes, I wished it were my dad who had gotten sick. Maybe if he had gotten sick instead of Brendan's dad, he would've seen things differently. He wanted me to join the football team at school that year. He said it would toughen me up.

"I played in school," he said one night while brandishing a forkful of leftover meatloaf at me. "Best thing I ever did. That's how I met my best friend."

I told my dad that I wasn't going to join, but after several long talks during breakfasts and suppers, I gave in and joined the team and I'd never seen my dad look happier.

Practice was held every day after class. For the first few days, we had to practice in the gym because the grass was muddy from all the rain we had gotten that year. Much to my dismay, I quickly learned that Michael Evans was the star of our team and I had to listen to him gloat and laugh for several hours a day at practice.

My coach always pretended that he didn't hear Michael. He was a large, rounded man with a bald head and a face that was always red. Whenever he raised an arm, there was always a yellow blotch on his shirt where his underarms were. He spat when he talked, too, which is why nobody got very close to him when he spoke, especially when he was mad.

"Run the damn ball, you hear me? Don't be such fairies out there!" he shouted one day, when we were standing in a huddle during our first scrimmage with Stroudsburg.

When the huddle broke, I headed over toward the bench, where I normally sat and watched Michael Evans on the field. As I walked with my head down, Michael clapped me on the shoulder. When I looked up, I

72

saw that he had that same, smug look on his face that he'd had in the Freak Tent.

"Some people can't help looking like fairies, huh?"

My eyes narrowed. "What's that supposed to mean?"

He laughed. "I wish I had a camera with me in that tent. Ya know? I wish I could show everyone that look on your face when you shat your pants in there."

My knuckles turned white around the helmet I was holding. I opened my mouth to respond, but I was interrupted by the coach, who had waddled over in his haste to get the game going again.

"Evans!" he shouted. "Get the hell out there!"

Michael gave me another smirk before hurrying onto the field. Several cheerleaders screamed through megaphones and tossed their pom poms into the air as he took the field.

* * * * *

I rode my bike past Brendan's house every day after practice, hoping he'd be looking out of his window. My Dad didn't want me to see him anymore and he wasn't in school because he was supposed to spend time with his Dad. I'm not sure what was going on inside that house of his. The curtains were always drawn and the grass of the front yard, once green and lush, was now turning brown.

He wasn't answering any of my calls. Nobody was. The phone would just ring and ring until I'd hang up because my mom was trying to pull it from my hands because she wanted to gossip with Mrs. Samuelson about Mrs. Veronica's divorce.

"Give it here!" she said quickly one night, accidentally scratching me with her nails as she took the phone. "Oh, honey! I'm sorry! I'm just *bursting* to tell Mrs. Samuelson about something. I'll be done by seven."

73

As I walked away from the phone, I remembered the last time I'd seen Brendan a few weeks earlier. On my way out the door, my Dad had stopped me to say, "Hunter, you don't have to be friends with him just because you feel bad for him."

"I'm not his friend because I feel bad for him. I'm his friend because I like him."

"You have new friends now, don't you? Why don't you hang out with the other boys on the team? I bet you'd like that. They're nice boys, all of them. You have so much more in common with them, don't you think?"

I raised an eyebrow. "What does that mean?"

He sighed. "Brendan just isn't like the other boys. Don't be his friend because you pity him. That's worse than not being his friend at all. You can still be nice to someone without being their friend."

* * * * *

One miserable rainy day, I was sitting at the breakfast table and I realized that I hadn't seen Brendan in nearly two weeks. Afterward, I got really sad when I thought about it and finished my cereal without even eating all of the marshmallows.

I don't understand how things happen. I don't understand where people go, or why things change. Brendan meant a lot to me, because around him, I'd always be that boy who shivered because the water of the sprinkler was too cold. He was the only person in the world who made me feel young and like the future was going to be full of sunshine and long, warm summers. Despite the memories, I found myself riding my bike past his house less and less because I was sick of staring at closed curtains. I stopped calling him as much because I couldn't bear to keep hearing the phone ring endlessly.

74

"Sometimes, you need to let things go," I whispered to my reflection in the mirror while wiping my eyes. "It's just for right now. He just needs time, that's all."

And I tried to believe it, because Brendan reminded me of long bicycle rides and lemonade stands, and although he wasn't dead or gone, seeing closed curtains was ruining everything that ever was.

Schoolwork picked up and our team ended up going to the state championship that year, so everyone was always trying to talk to me about that. Nobody was happier than my Dad, who sometimes made me breakfast on the weekends to celebrate. When he sat me down in the living room to watch the games with him, I learned to curse and yell at the screen when things went wrong. The first few times, when I didn't, Dad got really mad and told me that I wasn't appreciating the time he was trying to spend with me.

I didn't hear from Brendan until my birthday. I was sitting in the kitchen with my Dad, who was paging through a stack of mail. He had heated up some TV dinners for us both because it was late and Mom was upstairs sleeping off a headache.

"Did your mother give you your birthday money yet?"

"She did this morning."

"How much?"

"Twenty."

He nodded. Afterward, he tossed a white envelope across the table.

"You got something from somebody."

It spun to a halt several inches from my hand. I didn't recognize the handwriting at first, because it was written in cursive.

"I... I got a card? But I thought—"

He began picking at something in his teeth. "Open it."

I ripped open the envelope and a birthday card slid onto my lap.

"Who's it from?"

I opened it to find a five dollar bill.

After several moments, I said, "Aunt Margarette."

My dad nodded and then stood up from the dinner table. "I didn't even know she remembered our address."

And as he turned his back to me and dumped the dinner into the garbage, I smiled and opened the card again. There was a drawing inside of a Ferris Wheel. Beneath it, a message was written.

"Happy Birthday, Hunter. Love, Brendan."

The Night I Wore A Clown Mask

The first snowflakes began to fall outside. Football practice grew longer, even though the days were shorter because the state championship was less than two weeks away. Every night, I'd come home and my mom would take my pads and pants and try to scrub away the red stains from the grass. She'd drift in and out of the laundry room while talking to my father, who never listened anyway. A few times, she accidentally dropped her glass of wine and my father would slam his fist into the wall and call her "butter fingers." One night, my dad even needed to go get stitches because he cut up his knuckles really badly from hitting the wall too hard.

While my dad was shouting that day and gripping his bleeding hand, I thought of Gabriel and how he used to punch the bed posts. Afterward, I thought about Brendan, and although it usually made me sad to think about him, it was okay this time, because I hid his birthday card inside a drawer upstairs beneath my old pajamas. They had rocket ships on them which was the reason that I kept them. My mom was going to throw them away one day, but I cried, so she let me keep them.

One night, when football practice crept past seven, I found a bunch of stuff at the bottom of my gym bag that hadn't been there before. Michael Evans was the only person who could've done it because everyone else had left, even the coach, who was reluctant to do so, but needed to meet his wife for dinner at some fancy restaurant that I couldn't picture him going to.

At the time, I'd wondered why Michael hadn't left practice right away, instead, deciding to run a few laps around the field. When he watched me dump all the stuff from my bag into the trash can, I knew that he'd only stayed because he wanted to see my reaction to what he'd put in there.

77

"Don't throw them away!" he called. "You're going to need them soon!"

I tried to ignore him because I didn't know what he meant, but he came really close and whispered in my ear, "You know what those are, right?"

I nodded, even though I didn't. He knew I was lying and laughed.

"You stick them up your pussy so you won't bleed all over your pants."

"What?" I stammered. "What did you say?"

"You stick them up your *pussy*. P-U-S-S-Y."

"Shut up, Michael."

"Don't you remember? Back in the tent? Didn't you see the blood between that fat girl's thighs? Bet she would've *loved* one of these..."

"Shut up!" I said again, this time more forcefully, before I shoved him really hard and he almost fell onto his backside.

"Did you hear what's gonna happen?" he laughed. "Just down the road from your house?"

I shook my head.

He tried to hide the high-pitched cracking of his voice, but the giddiness broke through. "You didn't see? At the bottom of your bag?"

I plunged my hand to the bottom and searched around until I felt something cold and waxy.

"What did you...?"

I pulled it out and saw what it was— a rubber clown mask.

Michael cackled and came really close. "Are you gonna come? You're a tough guy now, aren't ya?"

My eyes narrowed. "Come to what?"

"All of the older boys are going to be there. You should be there, too. Prove that you're just like them."

"What do you mean? I... I *am* just like them."

"They're meeting on the tennis courts at nine. Bring a bat and wear the mask."

My eyes shifted from the eyeless mask to Michael's eyes, which looked just as empty.

"What are we gonna do?"

"We're going to do the kind of stuff you only see on television late at night. That stuff. You didn't think all the fun had to end when that carnival left town? This is the *real world* now. And just think…. we don't have to pay a quarter to have fun anymore."

Then, he tossed a few tampons at me that he had retrieved from the ground and began to head home. I heard his laughter from fifty feet away.

* * * * *

"Where are you going?" my brother asked me that night in the kitchen. His eyes traced the outline of the clown mask that I'd shoved into the pocket of my jeans. Afterward, his eyes flashed over to the baseball bat that I was holding and he got really excited because he thought I was going outside to play in the backyard.

"Pitch it slower this time!" he said, leaving the television on and skating past me so he could put his shoes on.

"No, Jamie, I can't play with you right now."

He skidded to a halt and his face fell.

"You can't?"

I sighed. "Tomorrow night, okay? I have to go."

For a moment, he examined my face because he knew that I was about to do something that I shouldn't. "Tomorrow night then," he whispered. "Don't forget. Soon, it'll be too cold to go outside at all and there will be too much snow."

"Yeah, I won't forget."

79

I slid out the door and headed down the front lawn. When I turned, I caught Jamie staring at me through the window. Once he finally disappeared, I forced the clown mask onto my face and hurried onto the street.

I passed Brendan's house on the way to the tennis courts. I waved at the upstairs window as if Brendan were looking down at me, even though he wasn't and the curtains were closed. For whatever reason, waving to the empty window made me feel better than walking by without doing anything at all.

It didn't matter that Brendan wasn't there to see me. He wouldn't have recognized me anyway. All he would've seen was a boy wearing a clown mask. Maybe he would've been afraid or maybe he would've just thought that I was Tommy Swanson's ghost.

Wouldn't that have been wonderful? I thought to myself. *Seeing Tommy Swanson waving at me from outside of my window?* And suddenly, I felt really guilty, because I fantasized about kissing Tommy Swanson beneath his clown mask and then running away with him to a different place and time.

The Night I Broke A Mailbox And Michael's Nose

When I got to the tennis courts, I saw a small huddle of nearly a dozen older boys smoking cigarettes through the holes of their rubber masks. One of them hollered when they saw me approaching.

"Hey! We got another one!"

"Where? I don't see nobody," I heard another voice say.

"Right *there*! He's coming up the goddamn path!"

As I approached, an overweight boy in an ugly turtleneck kicked open the gate to the court and bowed.

"Welcome, welcome," he said, grabbing me by the hand and ushering me to the center of the court. Before I could stop him, he pulled the bat from my hands and examined it.

"*Jesus*. This has an autograph on it..."

I didn't answer at first because I was too busy trying to find Michael in the crowd. "It's my Dad's."

"*Al Rosen*... you ever meet him?"

I was about to lie and tell him that I did, but another one of the boys stepped forward. "Better keep a close eye on that bat you got there," he told me, taking the bat from the boy in the turtleneck and returning it to me. "Albie's got sticky fingers."

I smiled dumbly, although nobody could really see it through the mask, and a third boy, one who was chewing on a toothpick, asked me for my name.

I told him the first name that I could think of. "Tommy."

"Is this your first time going for a ride with us?"

I nodded.

"How'd you know where to find us? We don't post this shit in the paper."

I cleared my throat. "My... *friend* said you guys would be here."

"Who's your friend?"

That's when I heard a familiar voice. "It was me."

All eyes flashed to Michael, who stepped forward.

"I told him we'd be here."

The boy with the turtleneck crept forward, cracking his knuckles. "Aw man, we got a *virgin*."

The boy with the toothpick chuckled. "Let's show our new friend a good time tonight then, alright boys?"

All of the boys nodded in unison. One of them clapped me on the back. Another shook my hand. I followed them through the gate of the tennis court and toward the street, where a car was parked beside a few bicycles.

The boy with the toothpick took the driver's seat. I sat beside Michael in the back, who elbowed me really hard in the ribs. He chuckled when I didn't make a noise because he knew that I was afraid to.

The boy in the turtleneck plopped down into the passenger seat and gave a thumbs up to the remaining boys on the street. "We'll meet you there. Five, thirty-seven. Cardinal Road."

They nodded and disappeared down the road.

I don't remember much about the drive to 537. Michael didn't say anything, and all that I could hear was the obnoxious, raspy voices coming through the radio that talked about sex and women.

The car reeked of alcohol and a pungent odor that smelled like cat pee. The open window didn't help much— it just made my eyes water really badly. Or maybe they were still watering because Michael had elbowed me in the ribs. I couldn't tell.

The car stopped on a road that didn't have any streetlights. The cement sides of the townhouses were cracked and broken like the macadam of the basketball court across from my house.

House 537 had a window with a broken screen and black scuff marks down the white paint of the front door.

"Are we going in there?" I asked Michael, suddenly nervous because the house looked like it belonged in a horror movie.

He smirked. "No, he'll be coming out here."

The car engine groaned to silence and we all got out. Behind me, I heard a cackle from down the road and I turned to see the other boys arriving on their bicycles. One of them rang the bell on the handlebars and circled around us. I recognized his laughter. He was the boy who had spat in my lemonade a few years ago.

"Let the new guy start it!" he shouted, pointing at me. "I want him to do it!"

I swallowed hard as the bicycles skidded to a halt a few feet behind me. Michael Evans nudged me closer toward the house.

"I don't know what you want me to do," I stammered, but Michael pushed me again.

Somebody behind me laughed. I felt my hands get sweaty and my face get red. I tightened my grip around the baseball bat. Then, I heard somebody whisper in my ear and I saw the toothpick from the corner of my eye.

"You see that mailbox?"

I nodded.

"Smash it."

I turned, surprised. "What? You want me to... smash it?"

Michael Evans sighed impatiently. "That's what he said. You're not deaf, are ya?"

My gaze shot from mask to mask. All of the boys watched me without blinking. There was an excitement in their eyes— one that I hadn't seen in a long time.

"Okay," I mumbled, but I'm not sure if anybody else heard.

I stepped forward, licked my lips and then...

Smash!

There was cheering behind me.

Smash! Smash!

As I swung again and again, trying not to think about what I was doing, the other boys scattered around me like ants. Some of them swung their bats through the house's windows. The other boys climbed onto the roof of the car in the driveway. Somebody began hitting the windshield while, beside him, the boy with the toothpick wrote "NIGGER" across the back bumper in red spray paint.

Shocked, I let the bat fall from my hands. It clattered against the street and rolled a few feet away from me.

And everything that followed happened so fast. A light in the upstairs windows flickered on and we heard a scream from inside the house. Michael, who had been pissing across the front porch, grabbed a handful of stones and whipped them at the front door.

"Leave, you damn ape!" he called.

Moments later, whoever was screaming at us from the upstairs windows threw a beer bottle down at Michael. It shattered on the front walkway.

"God damn ape!" Michael shouted. "You're lucky you didn't hit me or I'd—"

Michael fell silent. A siren had sounded in the distance and everybody turned to face one another.

"Shit!" one of the boys shouted. "We gotta go…"

The siren grew louder. I didn't have a chance to grab my bat before leaving because Michael pulled at my arm and nearly dragged me onto the street.

"Come on!"

Behind me on the street, I heard the roaring of an engine. The boy with the toothpick had hopped into his car and peeled down the road without waiting for anybody else to get inside. Some of the remaining boys leapt onto their bicycles and disappeared into the darkness. Others took off on foot.

"Hunter! *Hurry up!*" Michael shouted from across the street.

I began to run after him. I shot another glance over my shoulder when I heard the front door of the house come crashing open. For a moment, I caught sight of a large figure in the doorway. The man's skin was dark. That's all that I remembered.

* * * * *

Michael and I ran as fast as we could until we were back in my neighborhood, panting and collapsing onto the cold cement of the tennis courts. Once Michael regained his breath, he started laughing. "Did you see his face? Christ, that was good."

I pulled off my mask and shoved it back into my pocket. "What did he ever do?" I asked breathlessly.

Michael's eyes flickered over to mine. "He works at the A&P. He's a bagger. Probably too dumb to even work the register."

"What did he ever *do*?" I asked again, this time louder.

Michael rolled his eyes. "Don't be such a pussy. That was *fun*. People don't know their place and it gets them into trouble. Him and his big, fat smile. God, it's disgusting. Yellow teeth and everything. He was talking to my sister, ya hear? He was talking her up at the A&P like he had *the right* to."

I suddenly felt really sick and dirty, like I had when I saw all those faces inside the Freak Tent. I remembered the smell and the taste of the air in there. I remembered it all— the way my stomach churned and the way the arms and hands sounded when they were met with the blocks of concrete.

"Those apes," Michael continued, "Sometimes, I even catch some of them trying to drink from the same water fountain as us. Can you imagine? That'd be the day. They're all goddamn mad."

"I have to go home."

"Oh, I knew you'd be a bitch tonight!" Michael grumbled. "If you want to be my friend, you can't act that way."

And I was surprised that Michael had used the word "*friend.*" His voice softened a little bit when he said it, since we were alone and he wasn't putting on a show for anybody. I wondered, for the first time in my life, if Michael Evans was... *lonely.*

"I don't think we'd ever be friends..."

"Yeah," he mumbled, rising to his feet. "Because you're too much of a pussy about everything. And what the hell was the Tommy thing about?"

"It was the first name I could think of."

"Why didn't you say your real name? Why'd you have to lie to everybody?"

I started for the gate. "I don't know. Listen, I have to go home--"

"Wasn't he that kid? The one who hanged himself right across the street from your house?"

I stopped walking.

"Some of the boys knew him," Michael continued. "They said he was a flit."

"What did you call him?" I said, turning.

"A flit. F-L-I-T."

"Don't call him that."

"Why do you care? You didn't know him."

"I did. He used to cut my lawn. Sometimes, when he was doing it, we'd play this... this *stupid* little game..."

My voice faded to silence because I knew I sounded dumb.

Michael laughed. "He probably wanted to touch you. That's how those people are."

I clenched my jaw. "Don't say that."

His laughter grew louder. "He did a good thing that morning that he died."

"Michael, shut up…"

"He probably knew he'd start touching kids if he didn't off himself."

"I said *shut up!*"

I shoved Michael really hard and he nearly fell to the concrete. Once he regained his balance, he came at me. He pushed me to the ground, but as I fell, I grabbed hold of his shirt and pulled him down with me. We both rolled around for a few minutes while we swung at each other.

When we finally broke apart, Michael was making a really strange noise, almost like he couldn't breathe through his nose. When he finally pulled off his clown mask, I saw that his face was bloodied. He didn't know it at first, but he tasted it on his lips and cupped his hand around his nose.

"My… my nose!" he said, his voice more nasally than usual. His eyes were watering really badly, and I knew he was afraid that I'd see him cry. So instead of trying to shove me again, he just spat, "You know what, Hunter? Go *fuck* yourself."

And it was the first time I ever heard that word. Fuck.

But I wasn't thinking about that. I was thinking about his bloody nose, and how he looked almost exactly the same with the clown mask on as he did without it.

With the image burned into my eyes, I turned toward the gate of the tennis courts. "I… I need to go…"

"Where the hell are you going?" he shouted, still nursing his bloody nose. "You coward!"

"I'm not a coward," I scoffed while limping away because I had fallen wrong on my knee.

"Then why are you afraid to have another go at me? Huh?"

"I'm not afraid. Just shut up and go home."

"If you tell me that one more time, I swear I'm gonna-"

"Michael! *Shut the hell up!*"

Before I could take another breath, I heard footsteps coming toward me. I was about to turn, but I felt something hard collide with the back of my head. I felt my knees buckle and everything around me went hazy and black.

"Fucking poof," I heard Michael mumble as I fell to the concrete. Soon after, I heard the sound of his baseball bat clattering to the ground beside me. Something warm hit the side of my cheek, and I realized that Michael had spat on me. "I warned you!" he called, his voice growing fainter because he was running away from me. "Get bent, you goddamn poof."

The sound of his footsteps vanished. Now, all that I could hear was a soft ringing somewhere in the back of my head. I let my eyelids close, because they felt too heavy to keep open.

Darkness. It was all that I could see apart from a few fireworks that burst across my eyelids. At first, I couldn't tell if they were real or not, but after a moment or two, I realized that the fireworks were just the veins across my eyelids.

Boom! Another firework. If they weren't real, why could I hear them? I even felt the vibration in the ground. Then, everything was peaceful. I had no worries. I had no pain. The winter air was cold, but it felt refreshing on my sweating face.

That was when I felt something new and strange.

It made me laugh. Not out loud, of course, because I couldn't move my mouth. It began as a slight tickle down my arms and legs. I didn't know what it was, because I couldn't see anything, but as the sensation traveled further down my body, I started to panic. I imagined millions of spider legs against my skin, and the thought of that made me scream and shout.

My eyes snapped open. It took me several moments to realize that it was snowing. The tennis court was blanketed with white and the trees just outside the gate were covered, too.

"You're awake," I heard somebody whisper.

My heart fluttered. I could see him now— a boy standing overtop of me, but it was too dark for me to make out who he was. My eyes traveled from his face to his arms and then down to his hands, where I could see that he was cradling something in his palms. When he moved a little closer, that's when I realized what he was holding.

White roses. Whoever was standing overtop of me had placed dozens of roses all around my body.

"Here… let me get this for you," the boy whispered. He knelt down beside me and brought one of the roses to my face. He wiped my cheek until it was clean and I could no longer feel Michael's cold saliva dripping into the crevices of my neck. "There, kid. You're good as new."

I fought for words, but the boy put a finger to my lips.

"Shhh, it's okay. Just go back to sleep. You're all right, I gotcha."

"*Tommy,*" I choked out.

And at the sound of his name, I could've sworn he almost smiled.

"Christ," he mumbled, looking down into my eyes. "Don't cry. What are you, a baby?"

A few tears glided down my cheeks. "*Tommy…*" I whispered again. "Are you…"

He sighed. "I never thanked you for those stupid flowers. So, to make up for it, I made sure you were safe tonight. Now, I can get you out of my goddamn hair."

I tried to move my lips again, to say something more, but nothing came out and Tommy just shook his head and stood.

"Besides, I told you all of my secrets while you were asleep."

He pulled a cigarette from the waistline of his underwear and twirled it around in his fingers. "Can I tell you another one? While you're awake?"

"*Tommy... are you...?*"

He put the cigarette into his mouth. "The rope I used to do it... it was one that I found in your shed. Did your dad ever tell you that?"

And I imagined it in my head and it made me cry, just like I did four years ago when I saw him on the playground.

"Tommy, are you... *real?*"

But as I said it, he disappeared and so did the white roses. My eyes snapped closed again and the fireworks across my eyelids returned and I dreamed some more about Tommy's voice. Somehow, it kept me safe as I was lying alone that night on the empty tennis courts.

The Morning Brendan's Dad Was In The Obituary

I didn't realize that I had Michael's blood on the back of my hand until I had gotten home. Jamie had left the television on for me and in the white glow of the screen, I could see the blood glistening like the firework stamp they'd given me at the carnival.

That's what I thought it was at first. I almost started to cry because I thought it had come back after all this time.

The following morning, Michael's mother called my parents to tell them about how I had nearly broken Michael's nose during our fight the night before. I was sitting at the breakfast table beside Jamie when I heard the phone ring. My father answered, and while he paced around the room and listened to Mrs. Evans, he kept throwing glances my way. Suddenly, I wasn't hungry, so instead of eating my bowl of cereal, I stirred my spoon around in the soggy mess and tried not to make eye contact with my dad.

I knew that I was going to be in trouble because a few times, my dad apologized and said he'd cover the medical bills. The longer they talked, the sicker I felt, until I could've sworn I was going to throw up into my bowl of cereal.

After my dad hung up the phone, he asked me what happened. He was really calm when he asked, and that seemed to annoy my mom. I lied and said that Michael called me a girl when we were playing a game of neighborhood football the previous night at the field by the crick. By the time I had finished my story, a really big smile had swallowed my dad's face, almost like he won the lottery or something. He looked at the large bruise on the back of my head from Michael's baseball bat. He pressed down on it and I nearly choked.

When he was done, he shrugged. "He shouldn't have antagonized you. He had it coming."

My mother frowned and my dad opened up the newspaper on the table. I heard him turning through the pages while I rinsed out my cereal bowl and then watched the raindrops slide down the window above the kitchen sink.

My dad sighed and spread out the paper. "That's a shame."

I almost dropped my bowl onto the floor because I knew that he was looking at a photograph in the paper of the house on Cardinal. I had seen the picture in there when I'd brought in the paper from the front porch. Earlier that morning, they were even talking about it on the news. The news anchor said something about how the black man who owned that house had fled town because, while the police were investigating, some little girl had supposedly come forward and said that the black man tried to touch her in the parking lot of A&P. For some reason, I didn't believe it.

"Such a shame," my father continued.

I looked over, afraid to ask. "What is?"

"What was that boy's name?"

"Whose?"

My dad didn't answer right away, because he was trying to figure it out himself. When he couldn't, he said, "Your... *old* friend's? He lives down the street."

I frowned at the blatant emphasis of the word "old."

"Are you talking about Brendan?"

My father nodded. "Yeah. That's it."

"What about him?"

"It says here that his father passed away yesterday morning."

I dropped my spoon and it clattered loudly against the bottom of the sink basin. "He did?"

"Died in his sleep. What a shame. That boy needed somebody to fill him out."

* * * * *

It was raining really hard that day, but I wheeled my bike out of the garage anyway. My tires sloshed through the puddles alongside the road as I rode as fast as I could to the other side of the neighborhood. I couldn't see very well because everything looked gray and the rain kept getting in my eyes.

I skidded to a halt outside of Brendan's house. For several long moments, I just stared at the windows. The blinds were drawn and the house was quiet.

And suddenly, something inside of me changed. I became very afraid. I wish I could've ignored the fear and had enough guts to walk up the front porch steps and ring the doorbell. If I'd done that, I could've cried with Brendan in the rain while lying in his backyard. There weren't any clouds to watch that day, but at least he wouldn't have been alone.

I wish I had done that. Really, I do, but death was still a stranger that I didn't understand and I didn't know what to do or say. All of the curtains were drawn and the house didn't look like I remembered it.

For some reason, that terrified me. The thought of going inside that house again made me feel like I had a stomach ache because it wouldn't smell like grass anymore and the air wouldn't be alive and fresh, but stale and filled with the scent of somebody sick and dying.

I didn't want Brendan's house to be ruined. In my head, it meant something-- something that I can't really describe. If I went in there again, it'd never look the same in my head again and I didn't want the greatest memories of my life to be ruined.

So instead of ringing the doorbell, I rode my bike back home. Instead of hugging Brendan and making things easier, I wheeled my bike to a halt in our cramped little garage. Instead of tying flowers around Brendan's mailbox like I'd done around the monkey bars, I crawled back into my bed even though I was wide awake.

The Nights I Visited Tommy Swanson's House

Tommy Swanson used to live on the cul-de-sac of Cortland Road. Most people in the neighborhood forgot the house existed because nobody ever drove past it unless they went out of their way to. Back when I was young, a few of the older boys used to go there in the middle of the night. They'd close their eyes and see who could stand on the front lawn the longest before getting scared. The record belonged to a boy named Scotty Preston. He lasted seven minutes and twenty-two seconds before he heard the rustling of bushes and leapt backward onto the sidewalk.

My record was much longer— but I never told anybody about it. In the weeks that followed the death of Brendan's father, I drove my bicycle to Tommy Swanson's house and stood outside of it the way that I stood outside of Brendan's house the morning that I found out that his dad was gone.

Tommy Swanson's lawn was beautifully manicured, and I always found that so strange. The grass was red, too, just like all of the other houses and that always made me angry.

One particular night, I snuck out while my family was asleep and stood on the front lawn of his house until nearly half past two. That was the day that they buried Brendan's dad in the cemetery across town. I didn't go to the funeral because I didn't want to see Brendan's dad dead in the casket.

To this day, I know that I will never forgive myself for not going. That's one of the biggest regrets of my life, but at the time, I couldn't bring myself to go. I couldn't stand the thought of looking at him with all that ugly makeup that they'd put on his face. Why do we do it, huh? Why do we let them bury our loved ones in that ugly clown makeup?

So that night, I stood on Tommy Swanson's front lawn until I was so exhausted, I could barely stand upright. All of the lights of the house were out and nobody was awake to see me. It was foggy that night, too, so nobody would've been able to see me even if they wanted to.

I was late to school the next day because I hadn't slept more than an hour or two. Our teacher brought in a reel that morning and played it to the class. That day, Michael was sitting two seats in front of me. While Mrs. Applebee fumbled with the projector, I could see him daring a few of the other boys to pinch her ass.

Before anybody could, she turned around and somebody in the back of the room flicked off the lights and a title card appeared across the blackboard. It read: "IS IT TIME TO MOURN?" After fading to black, we saw a clown lying with his eyes closed before a tombstone that read, "HERE LIES YOUR CHILDHOOD."

After a moment, the clown winked at the camera and then cackled. "Oh, your childhood may have ended, but weren't the swings getting boring?"

The clown cleared his throat, pulled a long stream of colored ribbon from his mouth, straightened his tie and then continued. The camera cut to a man handing out ice cream cones to excited boys and girls.

"All of your life, you bought popsicles and ice creams. You ate all of them up, and boy, did they taste good. But now, kiddos, it's time you start selling them instead."

Money. It was everywhere. The children were thrusting dollar bills into the ice cream man's hand. He was smiling and wiping the sweat from his forehead.

The scene cut to a fortune teller's tent. The clown picked at his teeth with a splintered popsicle stick while a woman dressed in robes peered into a crystal ball.

"Now, I may not be able to predict the future," the clown began, turning to the camera, "but ours looks *bright*. Adulthood doesn't have to be grim. I'll make you a promise, alright? I'll keep an eye on you. I'll make sure you're doing it right."

The clouds in the crystal ball disappeared and were replaced with crisp images of teenage boys and girls in school. The image shifted to a boy and girl walking down an alleyway before it showed them lying in their bedrooms. The clown, who'd been smiling into the camera, laughed and his beady eyes flickered back toward the crystal ball.

"Did you think I was just gonna disappear after the carnival? I care about you all too much! Kiddos, you and I... we're friends for *life*!"

* * * * *

I returned to Tommy Swanson's house every night that week. I'd sometimes stay so late that the following morning, I'd have deep bags underneath my eyes. My father kept feeding me more and more each day to give me energy because the football team had made it to states. He couldn't figure out why I was so tired, and I didn't dare tell him I was sneaking out in the middle of the night.

"Eat up," he said one morning, shoveling a pile of scrambled eggs onto my plate. "You look like a goddamn ghost."

I dug my fork into the pile of eggs, but wasn't hungry enough to eat anything.

"Only one week until the big game," he reminded me. "You ought to be in bed early this week, getting all the rest you can."

"I'll go to bed earlier, I promise."

"That a boy," he said with a smile, clapping me on the back. Afterward, he sat down across from me and unfolded the newspaper. He disappeared behind it and while he wasn't looking, I emptied most of my plate into the trash before rinsing the plate off in the sink. I snuck out of the kitchen before he could ask me if I wanted to throw with him in the backyard.

The following day, I caught Michael Evans in the school's weight room after football practice. He was hopping up and down and smacking his chest. At first, I thought he was staring at himself in the mirror, but I quickly realized that he was staring at the mural that the art club had painted across the wall above the weightlifting equipment.

Our coaches showed us that damn mural once a week. Our mascot was an angel— one with muscular arms and massive wings that were beautiful and golden. Beneath its feet, "THROUGH THESE HALLWAYS BEAT THE WINGS OF CHAMPIONS," was written in cursive.

Nobody believed in that mural more than Michael Evans. He'd stare at that thing for hours while he worked like he was actually talking to God or something.

And maybe he prayed a few times because we won states that year. I had been so exhausted that I dropped the ball once during the game, much to my father's dismay, who ended up screaming at me from the sideline and tossing his hat onto the ground and stomping on it. But regardless of my blunder, we won and Michael Evans kissed a large golden trophy and cheerleaders hollered and held up their stupid pom poms.

And that night, I visited Tommy Swanson's house and stared at it the way Michael Evans stared at the mural on the wall of the weightlifting room.

I'm not sure why, but it felt like a grave. He wasn't buried in the cemetery like Brendan's dad, so I had no tombstone to look at or cry in front of. Realistically, that's the only point of a grave— it gives people something to cry in front of.

And that's what Tommy Swanson's house became— a grave.

So that night, while I was staring at the front of his house, I became terribly curious and I know I shouldn't have done it, but I decided to slip through the gate and into the backyard. I'd never seen Tommy Swanson's backyard before, and while I walked around back there in the dark, I felt a tingling in my fingers and toes because I was nervous and excited.

There were apple trees back there that had lost all of their leaves because it wasn't summer anymore. Between two of them, I saw a rusted sprinkler that looked like it hadn't been touched in years.

So I touched it. I ran my fingers across the rough surface that was probably once pristine and shiny. Afterward, I touched the bark of the apple tree and ran my hand through the grass at my feet.

When I'd examined everything in his backyard two or three times, I felt sad. I was sad because it felt new and exciting and when I'd seen everything there was to see, I wanted more.

That's when my eyes traveled across the back of Tommy Swanson's house. The inside of the house was dark, but none of the shades were drawn on the second floor and I wondered which of the windows belonged to Tommy Swanson's room.

What did it look like? I wondered, drifting across the yard toward the house. *What did Tommy Swanson see every morning when he was alive? What did he see when he looked out his window?*

Then, there were more questions. *Was the bed made? Room clean? What did his wallpaper look like? What did the ceiling look like? Did he stare up at it at night like I did?*

I know it was stupid of me to think about those things, but I couldn't help it. Tommy Swanson felt so close to me when I was standing in his backyard. His memories were *there*, right in front of me, so I grabbed hold of the white lattice that had been bolted to the side of his house and climbed my way toward his window.

The higher I climbed, the more excited I became, until my arms and legs were trembling so badly, I almost lost my grip once or twice.

I pulled myself onto the small bit of roof outside of the second floor windows. As I did, the shingles on the roof scratched my knees really badly and made them bleed, but I could barely feel anything at all.

I'm not sure what I expected to see when I peered through the first window. For a moment or two, I couldn't see anything at all. When my eyes began adjusting to the darkness, I could see a nightstand and a mirror. Hungry for more, I pressed my face against the glass. That's when I heard a scream, and suddenly, I stumbled backward.

The scream sounded again and a light flickered on inside of the room. It cascaded through the window and blinded me. I tried to stop myself from sliding off of the roof, but there was nothing to grab onto, so I fell.

As I did, I heard a window open. Then, a girl's voice shouted, "Who are you?!"

I didn't have enough time to see the girl's face. Instead, I could just see the stars in the sky. When my back hit the ground, I thought that I was dead. My jaw clenched and I suddenly lost feeling in my arms and legs.

"What the hell were you doing?!" the voice cried again. "Looking through my window? Get outta here before I call the cops!"

But I couldn't move. I fought to stay conscious, but the harder I tried to stand, the less I could feel the ground. All at once, I couldn't see the stars anymore, but I could hear a new voice— one that sounded so beautiful that I couldn't help but smile.

"Who's there?!" Tommy called.

I tried to answer, but my jaw was clenched too tightly to move. When I tried to stand again, the only thing I managed to do was roll over onto my stomach until I was face down in the grass.

"What were you gonna do in there?!" Tommy demanded, anger in his voice. "You have no business here! Were you gonna steal? Was this some kind of dare?"

I tried to shake my head, but I'm not sure if Tommy could see.

"You're all the same!" he bellowed. "To all of you, I'm just a dare or a prank or… or a *scary story*! But let me tell you— I'm not just a story. I'm a boy, too! Just like *you*!"

He jabbed his finger into my back and I winced.

"I can *touch* you. Does that frighten you?"

"Tommy…"

"And if it's a scare you all want, it's a scare you'll get."

Suddenly, I could see fire. I couldn't move my neck, but I saw embers dancing in the wind.

"Are you afraid to die?" he asked with a hunger. "Do you want me to *hold your hand?*"

I rolled over again, onto my back. "Tommy… are you… *real?*"

And suddenly, his eyes grew wide. The anger left them and it was replaced with curiosity and wonder.

"Hunter? Is that you?"

At once, the fire vanished. I could no longer smell the smoke or see the dancing embers, but I could see a bright light ignite in Tommy Swanson's eyes.

"Were you *thinking* about me again?"

"Are you real?" I repeated, slightly weaker.

"Were you going into my room to look through my things? Nobody's been in there in ages."

He knelt down beside me and came inches from my face.

"Touch everything," he said, as if that would bring him back to life somehow. "Those things haven't been touched in years. Touch everything inside of that room because I just want all of my favorite things to be touched again."

And suddenly, Tommy Swanson was gone. I came back to consciousness and my head hurt worse than it had when Michael Evans had smacked it with the baseball bat. I staggered to my feet and spun around, searching for Tommy Swanson in that overgrown backyard, but he wasn't anywhere to be found.

Suddenly, I heard screaming again. I wheeled around to see the girl, probably no older than fifteen, pointing out the open window.

"Get out of here!" she shouted. "Go!"

And before I had a chance to say anything, she began throwing things at me from her window. Moments later, I was hurrying through Tommy's backyard and I didn't stop running until I was panting on my front porch.

The Night I Met Jackie Swanson

Who was the girl who I saw silhouetted in the window? I knew she was Tommy Swanson's sister, but was she anything like him? Did she cry when her childhood ended, too? Or was she just like everybody else?

Her name was Jackie Swanson. Remember the green splatter on Tommy Swanson's t-shirt? The nail polishes that he mixed together belonged to her. I wondered if she missed him as much as I did.

The following week, I asked a few of the neighborhood boys about her when we were walking home from school together. One of them told me that she was stuck up, but he kicked at the ground when he said it, and I had a feeling it was because she'd turned him down once.

"How can I talk to her?"

"Talk to her?" he said with a snort. "Why do you think she'd want to talk to a boy like you? She's a year older, you know."

"I have to ask her something."

"If it's a date you're looking for, you're not gonna get one. I saw her around school with a boy named Harley. He has a mustache and everything— so I guess that's what she goes for."

"I don't want to take her on a date. I just want to talk."

He shrugged. "Well good luck. Harley will pound you if he sees you talking to her."

"I think I'll be okay."

He smiled. "Confident, huh? My sister and her hang around the drive-in every Friday. See if you can find her there."

* * * * *

Sunset Drive-In was always full of loud teenagers who kissed a lot and never really watched any of the movies. All of the boys wore leather jackets and the girls would look at them and giggle because they usually only saw the boys in school uniforms.

I'd been once or twice with my family when I was young. The grass was always littered with spilled popcorn and hamburger wrappers. The neon sign always had a letter or two burnt out.

When I went looking for Jackie Swanson that Friday night, the theater was playing Cinderella. It was so crowded that I could barely weave between the parked cars. A few times, drunken boys hollered and threw popcorn at me as I passed because I was blocking their view. I knew they didn't care about the movie. They just wanted to impress their girlfriends.

It took me ten minutes to find Jackie Swanson, and at first, I wasn't even sure if it was her. She was with a group of five girls and they were laughing and talking about boys when I approached their car.

I was nervous to talk to her, and before I tapped her on the shoulder, I reminded myself of what I'd planned to say to her.

"Um… Jackie?"

The laughter in the car stopped. All of the girls looked at me, and I couldn't help but feel embarrassed because I knew they were all older and I was afraid they were going to make fun of me.

She looked me up and down. "Do I know you?"

"No," I stammered, caught slightly off guard by how cold her voice sounded. "I'm Hunter."

I outstretched a hand. She didn't shake it.

"Do you think I could ask you something?" I said, immediately pulling my hand back.

"You know, you're interrupting the movie. Maybe later."

My eyes flickered from hers to the movie screen. The Fairy Godmother was transforming Cinderella's shaggy, torn dress into the beautiful red one that she wears to the ball.

"Come on," I encouraged, slightly impatient. "It'll only take a minute. I'll buy you an ice-cream."

"I'm on a diet."

She turned away and there was an awkward silence because she was waiting for me to leave, but I didn't.

I pointed up at the screen. "It's a kid's movie anyway, you're not gonna miss much."

She shot her friends a look of annoyance. Afterward, she thrust open the door and marched toward me. "You've got five minutes, you hear?"

I nodded. "That's enough."

I led her between the cars and toward the snack bar. She trudged behind me, stomping her feet as loudly as she could so that I would know she was annoyed.

"So, what the hell is this all about?" she asked when we were far enough away from the cars that nobody could hear us talking. When I turned to face her, I saw that her eyes had narrowed. "You're not gonna do something stupid, like ask me to your school dance, are you?"

"No," I said quickly.

I didn't convince her.

"I'm already going with somebody else," I lied.

"I'm sure she wouldn't be happy that you're following me around. Don't you think?"

I outstretched a hand, ignoring what she said. "Are you going to shake my hand now that we're away from your friends? I'm Hunter."

She rolled her eyes but shook my hand. "Jackie, but you already know that, I suppose."

"I do."

"How?"

I took a deep breath. "Because I want to talk to you about Tommy."

Silence. She took a moment or two to digest what I said, and at first, she looked at me like she heard me wrong.

"Did you just say…?"

"Tommy Swanson. Your brother. I want to talk to you about him."

She nodded. I had a feeling, in that moment, that she was suddenly more interested in me than I was in her. When she spoke again, she sounded suddenly hopeful, despite her attempts to hide it. "What do you know about him?"

"Not a lot."

"Did you find something?"

"No."

"You can tell me. I won't tell anybody."

"Jackie… I was hoping you could tell me about *him*."

Her hope deflated and her cold exterior returned. "So, you don't know anything?"

"No," I admitted, and I could tell she was disappointed. "I thought you'd be able to—"

"I have to get back to my friends."

She tried to brush past me, but I grabbed hold of her arm. She spun around, offended, so I released her.

"Why the hell would I tell you anything? Everybody wants to know about what happened the night my brother died. Everyone cares about that, but did you even care about him? When he was alive?"

"Yes," I said dumbly. "He was the boy who always cut the lawns in the summer. Sometimes, we would play this game…"

Her eyebrow rose. "You'd play a *game*?"

"I know it's crazy. I know you don't know me, and I don't want to upset you, but for whatever reason, I miss him. I miss him and I don't know why."

She snorted. "How can you miss somebody you barely knew?"

I opened my mouth to respond, but stopped myself. To be honest, I didn't know what to say because I didn't even know the answer.

"That's what I thought," she said, pulling a cigarette from the pocket of her skirt. I watched her light it as I thought of what to say next.

I swallowed hard. "Can I tell you something if you promise not to get mad?"

She shrugged. "I can't make that promise."

"Fine," I said, taking a deep breath. "I was the boy who you saw outside of your window last Tuesday night."

She furrowed her brow. After a moment or two, she recoiled a bit in disgust. "If you don't get lost, I think I might smack those dimples off your goddamn face!"

"I wasn't trying to look through your window," I said quickly. "I was trying to look through *his*."

"Why the hell would you want to do something like that?"

"I don't know," I stammered. "I just... I've dreamt about him since I was a little boy and I was there the day that he died. It was right across from my house and... I don't know... sometimes, I feel like he's trying to *talk* to me or something."

"*Talk* to you?"

I was suddenly embarrassed. My face must've gotten really red because I knew I sounded crazy.

She tossed her cigarette into the grass and crushed it with the heel of her shoe. "Well, since you're a *psychic* or something, next time he talks to you, tell him something for me, alright?"

"It's not like that..."

"Tell him we don't miss him."

I watched her brush past me and back toward her car. Suddenly, I was angry. I tried to calm myself down, but the harder I tried, the angrier I became. I stormed after her, and I know I shouldn't have said it, but I couldn't stop myself, and before I knew it, I grabbed her by the arm and said, "You know, I would've killed myself, too, if somebody like *you* were my sister."

She looked me dead in the eyes, and a moment or two passed where neither of us spoke, and then suddenly, she smacked me across the face. I could barely feel it. I'm not even sure if I winced, but I did manage to say, "He was your brother. How can you say something so goddamn *stupid?*"

She bit her bottom lip, ready to cry. Then, she whispered, "You're right. He was my brother. And the night that he died, I saw him leaving the house. He saw me on his way out the front door and he… he didn't even say *goodbye.*"

Suddenly, I wanted to take back what I'd said, even though I knew it was too late for me to do that.

"I found out about what he did when I pushed to the front of the crowd that morning and he was already… already *hanging there*! You think you have questions about the night my brother died? For every question you have, I have ten!"

"Jackie… I'm sorry… I didn't…."

Smack! She slapped me again.

Smack! And again.

Smack! And the third time, she grabbed hold of my cheeks and then held my face in her hands. Her voice softened to a near whisper. "You remind me a lot of him. You're *different.*"

And then, she let go of my face and turned around and that was the last time I ever spoke to Jackie Swanson.

The Night Michael Evans Became King Of The School

Different. Was it that obvious?

No, it couldn't be. I wouldn't let it be.

Two Friday nights later, my school held a dance with streamers and a punch bowl. I didn't want to go, but if I didn't go, I'd look different and it was only a matter of time before everyone noticed. I didn't know what I would do if they did, so I knew I had to try my best not to let them.

Besides, my mom got a fresh roll of film for her camera and bought me a nice white shirt and tie from the department store in town. I was going to the dance with a girl named Sally Chory. She was really pretty and had a smile that was as white as the clouds that I used to watch with Brendan. I knew that the dance wouldn't be terrible if I was with a girl like Sally, so I asked her if she'd go with me and she got really excited.

"Oh, isn't it just lovely? My *handsome* boy," my mom told me that night, running her hands across the creases in my dress shirt. "When will Sandra be here?"

"Sally," I corrected her, all the while, trying to push away her hands because she was just making the creases worse.

"You two better not try sneaking out without a few pictures first. We can finally replace those *awful* photos on the mantel from last year."

She was talking about the photos of me and Brendan— the ones that she insisted we take before our childhoods ended at the carnival. I looked ghostly pale. My eyes were sunken because I hadn't slept the night before and my hands were bunched into fists because I was nervous.

"I told you not to take those."

She didn't hear me, or maybe she did, but she was too distracted. She pursed her lips and backed away to examine my shirt.

"Oh, honey, don't you have a nicer belt? The leather's tearing on this one…"

"It's fine, Mom."

She began to fidget with my belt. When she accidentally scratched the top of my hand with her rings, I spat, "*It's fine, Mom!*"

For a moment or two, her face sank a bit. She pulled her hand back to her chest and awkwardly twisted her diamond ring around her finger.

To be honest, I felt bad because I knew she was trying to be a good mother. After a few moments, I didn't feel bad anymore because I knew she wouldn't remember any of this anyway.

"I'm sorry to make such a fuss. It's just… oh, it's your first school dance and I want it to be *perfect*."

I bit my tongue and thanked her. No matter how hard she tried, I knew that it wasn't going to be perfect. Brendan wasn't going to be there. Ever since his father passed, I hadn't seen him at school. I'm not sure if he was avoiding me or not, but it'd been nearly a month and a half and I hadn't seen him.

* * * * *

Thirty minutes later, Sally arrived in a beautiful white dress. My father answered the door and he seemed really excited that I was going to the dance with a pretty girl. He invited her into the den and asked her if she wanted anything to drink.

"No thank you," she smiled. "I'm alright."

"Are you ready to go?" I asked, trying to get out of my house as quickly as possible, but before she could answer, my mother came

109

hurrying over and fussed with my hair before pushing us together and snapping several photographs.

When my eyes were fuzzy from all of the flashes, I finally managed to convince my mother that we were late to the dance even though we weren't. I took Sally by the arm and we headed out the front door and down the porch stairs.

"Have a great time!" my father shouted after us.

"We will," Sally said with a wave. "Thanks for everything."

We began the long walk toward the school. I tried to make small talk with her, but I didn't really know what to say, and I couldn't tell if I was boring her or not. At one point, our hands got really sweaty since we were holding each other's, but I didn't want to take my hand away because I thought it'd hurt her feelings.

"Do you like to dance?" she finally asked, breaking a painful silence that had lasted between us for too long.

"I'm not much of a dancer, actually," I said with an uncomfortable laugh.

"You just have to get the hang of it," she told me. "Maybe you'll enjoy it."

"Yeah, maybe."

Silence again. I tried to talk about our classwork, and thankfully, she began to talk about a teacher that she didn't like and she didn't stop talking until we finally saw the lights of the school in the distance.

When we finally reached the front doors, I saw balloons and streamers decorating the hallway. Sally commented about how pretty they looked and I nodded. We hurried through the doors and toward the gymnasium, which was packed with boys and girls who were already dancing. A small band played terrible music in the corner and the temperature rose at least ten degrees when we stepped inside.

"I'll go get you some punch," I mumbled, releasing her hand and hurrying across the gym. As I went, I wiped my hand on my pants because it had gotten so wet and sweaty and I was relieved to give it some time to breathe.

My heart sank because Michael Evans was laughing and chatting with a few of his friends beside the punch bowl. When he saw me, he grabbed my arm and pulled me toward him.

"Hunter!" he said mockingly. His friends snickered.

"Hi, Michael."

"It's nice to see you here tonight. I haven't gotten a chance to talk to your mother in a long time."

His friends laughed again and I just looked at them all, confused. "What are you talking about?"

"She's your date, isn't she? You know what they say, right? You have a face only a mother could love…"

He ran his hand down the side of my face and I batted it away. "Very funny."

I turned away and reached for the ladle of the punch bowl. Before I could grab it, Michael snatched it away and a few droplets of punch splashed onto my face.

"Michael, come on. Give it."

"You want to have a good time tonight? How about you try some of the punch we made?"

He raised a plastic cup. When I brought it to my nose, it smelled funny.

"What's in it?"

"The stuff my dad likes. You can barely taste it. Try some."

I didn't want to. I was just about to give him back the cup when his friends sniggered again and Michael said, "See, I told you he wasn't going to drink it…"

So, I brought the cup to my mouth and took a generous swig. It reminded me of the rubbing alcohol that my mother had used to clean my cuts and scrapes when I was young. It burned the back of my throat and I couldn't stop myself from coughing really badly.

"How is it?" Michael asked, pouring himself a cup from a flask that one of his friends was hiding in the pocket of his suit.

"It's… good," I lied.

Michael smiled and raised his cup to mine. "Cheers, then."

When he took a swig, I took one, too. Before I knew it, I had finished the entire thing.

"I have to get back to my date," I said, wiping my mouth.

As I poured Sally a cup of the school's punch, Michael pushed another cup of his concoction into my hand. "Take one for the road."

I stared down at the murky red liquid. "Thanks."

And I left Michael and his friends sniggering at the table.

* * * * *

I didn't mean to finish the second cup. I'm not sure why I kept drinking it, but I felt really uncomfortable around Sally and every time an awkward silence came, I brought the rim to my mouth and took a gulp.

I wasn't sure if she knew what I was drinking or not, but she didn't say anything. I was terrified that if she got too close, she would smell it on my breath the way I always smelled it on my mother's. As much as I worried about that, I was even more afraid that she was going to look at me at some point for a moment too long and it'd dawn on her, then, that I'm… different. Would she know? What would she say?

I didn't know the answer, so I wasn't going to let her find out—even when she dragged me to the center of the dance floor. I felt awkward trying to dance with her. A few times, her eyes met mine, and I could've sworn she wanted to kiss me. Every time one of those moments came, I swallowed more punch and hid inside the cup for a moment or two.

112

Halfway through the dance, I started to feel strange. The music, which had initially sounded terrible, began sounding prettier and the lights above our heads became prettier, too. It was a wonderful feeling at first, but I started to feel dizzy after awhile and the lights began to sting my eyes.

Before I could think about it for too long, a terrible screeching sounded and everyone hollered and covered their ears. I looked around frantically and that's when I realized that Mrs. Applewood, the principal, had grabbed hold of the microphone.

"Good evening, students," she said, gazing around the room. "Are you having a good time?"

The crowd of students cheered. She continued to gaze around the gym, and somehow, her curly gray perm didn't move at all.

"I hate to interrupt, but it's time to announce our king and queen."

She licked her lips and a hush fell across the entire room. I felt Sally perk up beside me. She gave me a look of excitement, like it actually could be us, and I retreated back into my cup of punch, but much to my dismay, the cup was empty, apart from a few sour droplets at the bottom that tasted like cough syrup.

She grabbed hold of my arm and rested her cheek against my shoulder. "What would you do if it were us?"

I opened my mouth to respond, but for the first time, I felt sick. I wasn't sure where it came from, but I snapped my mouth closed and tried to swallow whatever was rising up my throat.

Mrs. Applewood gestured toward a rope that was hanging beside her— one that I hadn't noticed before. She twirled it around her manicured fingers. "And don't forget our king's duty…"

My eyes followed the rope up into the rafters above our heads, where I saw the dark outline of what looked like a large bucket.

She laughed. "And it's fresh— still warm even!"

There was applause. Suddenly, the boys on the dance floor started pushing their way to other ropes that were dangling just above their heads. I hadn't noticed them before either, and when I tried to get a better look at what they were tethered to, my head felt dizzy and I felt the punch rising up my throat again.

I took a deep breath. "What's up there? What's in those buckets?"

Sally looked at me, surprised. "You don't know?"

I shook my head, and as I did, I could've sworn the ground trembled for a moment.

"Did you hear me?!" Mrs. Applewood called. "I said it's *still warm!*"

More cheers. Suddenly, my legs felt weak. I tried to keep them steady.

"What's in them, Sally?"

"You're kidding, right?"

"No."

"It's why we all wore white."

"Tell me."

"Blood," she said with a laugh.

"What?"

"From the elephants. It's just like the slaughterings at the carnival! Remember? It's just like when we were young!"

Before I could respond, Mrs. Applewood was peeling open an envelope and licking her lips again. I shot a glance above my head, toward the darkness of the rafters. Frightened, I tried to push my way off of the dance floor, but the bodies were too close together and I couldn't get through.

"*MICHAEL EVANS AND HANNAH JONES!*"

Applause exploded. The band started playing again— louder than before. The music didn't sound sweet anymore. It sounded harsh and I felt it echo in my head.

"Hunter?"

Sally was trying to follow me through the crowd. I felt her hand on my arm and I brushed it away.

"Sally... I...."

"Hunter, are you okay?"

"I should get home..." I breathed. "I think I'm sick..."

"Sick?" she asked, her eyes widening, but I was so dizzy that I couldn't distinguish them apart anymore.

Just over her shoulder, I could see Michael Evans smiling and straightening a crown on top of his head. Mrs. Applewood smiled through her thin lips and handed him the microphone.

"Ladies and gentleman," Michael said, clearing his throat. "Your childhood may have ended, but *welcome to adulthood*!"

And he pulled at the rope beside him and the dozen other boys pulled at their ropes and I heard the buckets squeaking as they tilted down toward us— unleashing everything that was inside of them. For a moment or two, red blanketed us all. I squeezed my eyes shut so that I wouldn't have to see it, but that didn't stop me from feeling it. It was warm— just like Mrs. Applewood said. It was thick and smelled a lot like metal. It stung the corners of my eyes and danced across my lips. It was sticky— just like maple syrup. I could feel it trying to push its way inside of my mouth, so I tried my hardest not to scream or breath. Suddenly, the room went quiet and I felt the blood tunneling into my ears. I jammed my fingers into them as fast as I could so that no more blood could get inside.

When I finally opened my eyes, I could see everybody clapping and trying to catch the final droplets of blood in their hands. I turned back to Sally, who was watching me closely. I knew I was going to get sick, and I'm not sure if it was from the blood or from what Michael had given me to drink, but I didn't want to embarrass her.

"I'm sorry, Sally," I choked out.

"Are you okay?" she asked, even though I could barely hear her.

"I have to go…"

"Hunter—"

And as I turned away from her, she gave me a look— one that terrified me.

I'll never forget that look. As I pushed my way through the crowd, I saw that same look on everybody that I passed. It was a look of confusion, wonder, and maybe even a little bit of *pity*.

Do they know? I wondered. *Does everybody see it? How different I am?*

Behind me, the microphone made a terrible screeching sound because Michael let it fall to the ground. Beneath me, I could feel the blood beginning to soak through the soles of my shoes. Beside me, the boys kept twirling their girls and I could see the blood matting down their curls and settling in the crevices of their necks.

I finally managed to reach the gymnasium doors. Before long, I was pushing my way into the bathroom down the hall. When I looked at my reflection in the mirror above the sink, I saw that my eyes were sunken and the droplets on my face were already hardening around the outside. Immediately, I turned on the faucet and began scrubbing my face like I had scrubbed the firework stamp off the back of my hand after the freak tent.

As I did, I became too dizzy to stand. Before I could stop them, my legs gave out. I tried to grab hold of the side of the sink as I fell, but my hands were too slippery from all of the soap and blood.

I hit the floor hard, and when I did, I cried out in pain because one of my fingers bent the wrong way. I felt my throat opening wide, and as much as I tried to swallow it back down, the vomit came blasting out of my mouth and even through my nose. It was red— just like blood, and for a second, I got scared that I was bleeding somewhere deep inside.

"Help," I choked out weakly. "Help— can somebody help?!"

My eyes traveled across the floor, which looked like it was beginning to ripple.

"Help!" I called out again, but nobody heard me because the music was too loud.

I crawled into the nearest stall and vomited again before resting my throbbing head on the cold stall wall.

And that's when the darkness overtook my eyelids. I tried to fight that, too, because I wasn't sure what was happening, but it became too difficult. I gave into it. The last thing I remember hearing was Michael Evans' awful laughter.

"Welcome to adulthood! You hear me?! Let's make the most of it!"

* * * * *

When I finally came back to consciousness, I couldn't hear music anymore. Everything was quiet. My red vomit still swirled around the toilet bowl and looked a lot like that canned spaghetti that's shaped like alphabet noodles. When I closed my eyes, I felt the room spin and that made me vomit some more.

After several agonizing moments, I managed to breathe again. As I sat there, gasping for air beneath the flickering fluorescent lights, I heard the stall door creak open behind me.

"I'm... *fine*," I managed to choke out, slightly embarrassed that I was sprawled out so pathetically across the bathroom floor. Before I could say anything more, through the corner of my eye, I saw a hand pressing down the lever of the toilet.

I didn't look up because I was afraid I was going to see Michael Evans' sneering face and bad, greasy skin. Instead, I watched the water swirling around inside the toilet bowl.

Then, the silence came. I could still see the boy's shadow slanting across the floor, so I knew he hadn't left.

"You can go…" I whispered.

He didn't move.

I turned. "I said I'm *fine*."

And that's when I saw him.

"Get up off the floor, kid," he mumbled, grabbing hold of my shirt collar and pulling me to my feet. The pressure on my neck made me feel sick again, but I managed to keep everything down.

"*Tommy*…" I said, suddenly forgetting to breathe.

He started to dust off my jacket. "Too much to drink, huh? You better start looking after yourself. My dad used to drink, too. Liquor from Canada. Can you believe that? All the way from *Canada*."

"Tommy…"

"His bottles always said the liquor was *smooth*," he laughed, fixing my tie. Again, the sudden pressure across my Adam's apple made my throat open again, but I didn't want to be sick in front of Tommy.

When it finally felt safe to open my mouth without anything coming up my throat, I whispered between breaths, "What… are you…?"

"Doing here?" he laughed, finishing my thought. "I could ask you that, too."

I looked around. "It's… my school dance…."

He looked around, too. "A *dance*? Well, in that case…"

He put his hands on my hips and began to sway. I tried to move with him, but I could feel whatever remained in my stomach shifting around uncomfortably. A moment later, Tommy laughed and let go of my waist.

"Don't worry. I was never much of a dancer. Besides, the dance ended hours ago."

My eyes grew wide. "The dance ended already?"

He nodded. "But I didn't want your night to be a total bust, so I thought I'd come and ask you to dance. I thought you'd like that. We can dance for real, if you'd like."

"Dance for real?" I asked. My eyes traveled from his feet to his hands and then up and down his torso. I could see his chest rising and falling with each breath.

Tommy put his hand around my waist again. For a moment or two, he just looked into my eyes and I looked into his.

"I... I don't know how to dance..." I whispered meekly.

He pulled his hand away and laughed again. "Then I'll just dance in front of you."

And that's exactly what he did. He began to dance in front of me, and for the first time that night, I felt like laughing.

"You're smiling! Look at that!" he exclaimed.

He was right. Although my head ached and my stomach felt inside out, I was smiling. A few times, Tommy gave me a noogie— the kind I always used to give Brendan. When he did, my head throbbed, but I just kept laughed because I was still thinking about how Tommy danced like the boys did in the cartoons.

But when Tommy turned and caught sight of the mirror, he stopped dancing and I stopped laughing. From across the bathroom, we could both see blood droplets and bloody hand prints standing between us and our reflections.

For a moment, Tommy just stared at all the blood. I wondered what Tommy was thinking. *Was he thinking about how Brendan's dad used to bleed all over the bathroom sink and mirror, too?*

"Tommy?"

"You know, I knew him, too. I used to see him every Saturday morning— right between *Bozo* at seven thirty and *Huckleberry Hound* at noon. He'd always joke about how the top of his head was gonna be burnt as all hell by eleven... because, you know, his hair was thinning up there and all..."

When he tried to continue, his voice cracked. His eyes grew wide, and he look down at the ground so I wouldn't see him start to cry. All at once, he puffed out his chest and bellowed, "Go ahead! Call me a goddamn baby! I know that I am! I don't care. I just need to know how it happened. Christ, kid, he's *dead*. I wanted to leave with him, but I... I didn't know *how...*"

I suddenly felt a pain in my stomach because I remembered everything. I remembered how Brendan's house smelled like grass and how Tommy used to cut the lawns that Brendan's dad used to paint. In that moment, I felt sick again because I remembered what the photo of Brendan's dad looked like in the obituary. I remembered how my dad didn't save the newspaper for me that day even when I asked him to because I had wanted to put it with Brendan's birthday card beneath my rocket ship pajamas.

"He was always sick—" I whispered, trying to keep my voice steady.

"Everything is so... *messed up,*" Tommy stammered before running his hands through his hair and pacing up and down the bathroom. As he did, his breathing started to pick up, and before long, he was pulling at his hair and hitting himself.

"I just... I didn't know it was gonna happen!" he cried, throwing a punch at the wall. "How the hell was I supposed to know?! I would've been with him if I'd known!"

I tried to grab hold of Tommy's arms to stop him, but my arms were so weak that I could barely squeeze my hands closed.

"How'd it happen?" he continued. "That's the real reason I came— to ask you. I need to know. Was anybody with him?"

My eyes fluttered closed because the pain in my head had become too much again.

"How did he die?" Tommy demanded, turning around again.

"I... I don't know..."

"Tell me what you *do* know! Does he come to you at night? Do you see him in your dreams like you see me? Does he... *talk t*o you?"

I shook my head.

"Have you heard anything from his family?"

"He... died in his sleep..."

"Did he wake up in the middle of it? Did he know what was happening?"

"I don't know."

"How don't you know?!" he roared, kicking at the door to the stall. "Doesn't anybody pay attention? Doesn't anybody *look* to see what's going on?!"

I watched with a mixture of pity and horror as Tommy continued kicking at the stall door with his bare feet until his nails chipped and the tops of his feet broke open.

"I'll tell you what happened!" Tommy roared. "He probably woke up in the middle of it. He probably knew he was dying and... and *pissed* himself! He probably *pissed himself like I did*! Can you believe it?! I pissed myself like a *goddamn baby* because I was so scared and wanted my mother!"

When Tommy finally stopped kicking the door, he turned to face me, breathless. For several moments, he stared into my eyes and I stared back into his. Then, all at once, his face sank completely and he pulled me into a hug. "Christ, kid," he whispered through his tears, "I'm so sorry. I'm just afraid— that's all."

121

And even though I was frightened of Tommy and what he might do, I pulled him closer with what little strength I had left. "What are you afraid of?"

I felt his breath on the tip of my ear, followed by a few tears in my hair.

"I'm afraid he died all alone."

And then he pulled back, and I could breathe again.

"It just makes me sad," he whispered. "I want to stop being so *sad* all the time."

As he said that, I felt a sudden weakness return to my legs.

"I just want to be happy," Tommy continued. "And maybe you can help. Do you think you could help me, Hunter?"

"Tommy… I…"

"You know how I told you a secret on the tennis courts?" he asked meekly, his voice so low that I could barely hear it. "About how I used the rope from your shed? Can I tell you another secret? Right now?"

A shiver rolled down my spine. I began to feel my eyes closing again, and as they did, I sank back down to the floor.

Tommy hurried forward and caught me as I fell. "Promise you won't be mad," he whispered, his face only inches from mine. "It just made me so happy when I did it. I haven't felt that way since I was a kid…"

"Tommy…" I mumbled, trying to raise a hand to his cheeks, but before I could, my hand fell to the floor and my eyes closed completely. I couldn't see Tommy anymore. I tried to hold on, to stay awake, but the harder I tried, the further away his voice sounded.

And right before I lost consciousness, I felt Tommy Swanson squeezing my arms and pulling me closer.

"I know I shouldn't have done it, but Hunter, I kissed you that night. Do you hear that? I *kissed you*."

The Night Brendan Asked Me If I Believed in Heaven

When I finally awoke that night, the entire school was empty. My vomit still filled the toilet bowl and rolled down the side. I tried to clean it up with some paper towels, but the more I tried, the dizzier I became.

I finally stumbled my way out of the bathroom. The floor outside was sticky from the elephant blood that had been tracked out of the gymnasium. In the darkness, it looked a lot like melted tar.

The only light to guide me was the moonlight that slanted through the windows on the door at the end of the hallway. As I hurried toward it, I passed by the gymnasium doors, which were still open. The lights were out inside, so it was hard to see, but I saw that the round tables had been stripped of their tablecloths. The red balloons that had once been tethered to the backs of the seats were gone, too.

I'm not sure why I did it, because I knew he wouldn't be there, but I stumbled into the gymnasium anyway. The floor was stickier in there and hadn't fully dried yet.

"Tommy?" I asked, a twinge of hope still left in my voice.

No response.

"Tommy?" I asked again, this time louder. "Are you here?"

I spun around in the darkness a few times to check to see if anybody was emerging from the dark corners, but I saw nothing. I heard nothing. The only sound I could hear was my own breathing— which I realized was much louder than I meant for it to be.

"You said you were real!" I shouted, suddenly angry. "Prove it! Show yourself when I'm awake!"

I stumbled further into the gymnasium until I was standing at the base of the stage. The elephant blood was the thickest there, and as I hurried throughout the gymnasium, searching for Tommy Swanson, I slipped a few times and soaked my palms in the thickening blood.

"Come out you *coward*!"

Suddenly, I heard a shuffling sound from the corner. My heart skipped as I spun around, but sank again when I realized that it was just a paper banner rustling in the draft of an open window.

"Tommy?" I called one final time, my voice nearly breaking into a sob. "Tommy, *please*. I don't want to be alone right now..."

But he didn't answer me— nobody did. Tommy Swanson wasn't there. He was dead and wasn't coming back, and I was suddenly mad at myself for hoping for anything more.

I walked home alone that night. The streets were wet because it had rained earlier, and the oily puddles on the side of the road looked metallic and full of color beneath the streetlights.

At one point, I stared into one of the puddles for a long time because it looked just like a rainbow and I wanted to know if what Gabriel said three years ago was true. Was there green in the rainbow? When I finally saw the green, I bent over and dug my hand into the puddle and tried to cup it in my hands, but the moment I did that, the puddle lost its color. The blood washed off of my hands and clouded the water and made it look really ugly.

It was terribly strange, and I'm ashamed to admit it. Most people will never understand, but for whatever reason, as I stared into the red water of that puddle, for the first time in my life, I wanted to kill myself.

I continued to walk home with my head hung low. I don't remember a whole lot about that walk. The fresh air felt nice on my face, but I felt lonely because I passed by Brendan's house and it looked awfully dark and empty inside.

But I remembered a paper that I had tucked inside my pocket before leaving with Sally Chory for the dance. When I did, I walked over to Brendan's yard and did my best to wipe all of the blood onto his grass so that I wouldn't get any of it on his card. Then, I pulled it out of my pants pocket and tucked it inside Brendan's mailbox before hurrying home.

I never told anybody else what was on that card before. In its center, I drew a Ferris wheel. No words— just a Ferris wheel, because when I was up there with Brendan, it was the closest I'd ever felt to heaven.

* * * * *

Even with the dreams of Tommy Swanson and the sounds that my mom made with Mr. Roberts, I knew it was all going to be okay. Things were alright as long as that birthday card was still hidden beneath the rocket ship pajamas.

I hadn't seen him all that much, but I didn't need to. Because even with football and birthdays and his dad, we still had that promise. We knew we'd see each other every year, at the top of the Ferris Wheel at Barnaby's carnival.

"We're so high up," Brendan said that summer, with a light in his eye that made my insides hurt somewhere, deep down. But not a bad kind of hurt.

It was a summer filled with a hot stickiness that loomed in the air. There were clouds of dust, and the slight breeze carried the scent of animals from the petting zoo.

He looked uncomfortable and kept fiddling with his hands. At the time, I didn't know why. "Don't you ever get nervous?" he asked me, avoiding my eyes.

"Nervous about what?" I asked, watching the blinking fireflies all throughout the sky.

Brendan looked over the edge. "That this thing is just going to fall apart one day…"

I looked over the edge, too, and as I did, the ride rocked to a halt. We were halfway to the top, just high enough that we were level with the tops of the trees that outlined the fair boundaries. The gondola kept swinging back and forth as Brendan and I sat inside, staring down at the ground below where the hundreds of carnival-goers looked like ants.

I had needed to pass the Freak Tent to meet Brendan there that night. I saw all of the 13-year-old boys and girls. I saw their wide eyes. I heard the old woman saying, "*Name please! I need your name!*"

But I tried really hard not to look at any of it because I knew if I did, I'd dream about it at night.

Brendan spoke again, and I grew frightened because his voice sounded deeper than I remembered. "Mom says that they just get normal people off the street to throw these shitty things up. Some of them don't even have diplomas. Or at least, that's what she says."

I winced, but Brendan didn't notice. The ride began to turn again.

"Brendan? Can I ask you something?"

He didn't look over. He just nodded. When he did, I asked, "Why do you say things like that?"

His forehead crinkled in confusion. "Things like what? Mom says—"

"*Shit.* Things like that. You just said *shit* and you never used to say things like that before."

He thought about it for a few minutes, then shrugged. "I don't know. If you don't like it, I won't say it."

I shook my head. "No, I don't mind. I'm just curious, that's all."

He took a deep breath. "What are you curious about?"

"I don't know. Nothing, really. I shouldn't have said anything."

I could feel my body warm. It started in the tips of my fingers and spread down my arms.

"Brendan," I said again, my voice weaker. "Can I ask you something else?"

He gave me a nod, but before I could ask, the gondola rocked to a halt. We were at the top.

I took Brendan's hand. "Brendan…"

He bit his lip and smiled weakly. "Hunter."

Then, I leaned in. We began to kiss, and for those moments, I don't remember anything other than kissing him because there wasn't anything else that seemed to exist. Our kiss only lasted for a few moments before…

Brendan pulled back. His gaze shifted away from me again and he busied himself with staring over the edge of the gondola at all the people beneath us.

I grabbed hold of his hand again. I leaned forward, until my lips were brushing against his neck, but he backed away like he'd done before and I felt terribly cold.

"Why are you…"

Thunder rumbled somewhere overhead. Just beyond the tree lining, I could see dark storm clouds.

"I can't, Hunter."

"Listen," I whispered, stroking his hand, "I know that they say it's wrong, but I don't believe them and I really hope that you don't believe them either…"

Brendan kept watching the sky.

"My Dad…" he whispered. "He can see us now. He's watching from the sky and we're just so close to the sky up here. I just… I don't know anymore…"

I looked up at the sky, too. "Brendan, please…"

"He can see us here. This used to be the only place in the world where we could go, and nobody could see, but now, it's not like that anymore…"

"Please," I said again, this time more desperate. "Just this year. Just this once. I need this. Next year, I promise that I'll be stronger, so we won't have to."

There was a pause. Then, Brendan wiped his eyes and asked, "Hunter, do you believe in Heaven?"

The ride rocked back into motion. I grabbed hold of Brendan's hand, panicked, because I knew I was running out of time. Without really thinking, I leaned back in again, but I stopped myself before my lips could touch his because it didn't feel right anymore.

"Brendan.. I... I..."

And when the ride became still at the bottom, Brendan exited the gondola without waiting for me. He kept his eyes on the ground as he went, careful to avoid looking into mine because I think he was afraid it'd change something.

"Brendan!" I called. "Brendan, stop!"

I tried to grab hold of his arm, but he had already found his way into the crowded pathways. He turned back to face me slightly, almost like he had second thoughts, and I could see a tear slide down his cheek before more people stepped between us and I could no longer see him.

"Brendan!" I begged. "Brendan, *please!*"

But he was gone.

I spun around, unsure of what to do or where to go. All around me, people were laughing and enjoying their evening. I stood on tiptoe to try to see over everyone's heads, but there were too many red balloons in the way.

And when I finally gave up, I noticed somebody watching me from across the carnival path. When I realized that it was a clown, I quickly wiped my eyes and put my head down.

Had he seen it? Had he watched the entire thing?

I stole another glance. The clown was smiling— such a wicked smile. His lips looked ready to crack open on the sides. His face paint was different from the others. Beneath his left eye, I could see a blue crescent moon.

The clown's shoulders bounced up and down as if he were giggling. The last thing I saw him do before I ran away was raise his finger to his lips as if to tell me that he could keep a secret.

The Day My Father Hit My Mother For The First Time

Brendan meant something to me— something that I can't really explain. When I thought of Brendan, I thought about the way the grass smelled in the summer and the way the chlorinated water tasted when I was laughing really hard and the water from the sprinkler got into my mouth.

Did I ever tell you about those days? The ones where I used to run through the sprinkler with Brendan? Sorry if I have. It's just... those were the best days of my life.

I thought Brendan would never change. I thought he'd always be that boy who laughed because the sprinkler was too cold, but when I got home from the carnival that day, I had a feeling that Brendan was gone and that my childhood was gone, too. I couldn't keep either of them anymore. They both managed to slip through my hands and neither of them were coming back.

The sounds of a boxing match filled the house when I arrived back home. I could hear the cheering of a crowd and the sound of gloved fists colliding with skin and bone. A commentator's deep, excited voice echoed above the muffled applause.

"He has not even broken a sweat coming into this—"

And suddenly, above the shouting of the television, I could hear even more. I was sitting in the den, trying to focus on the black and white shapes on the television, but I couldn't ignore the shrieking and the shattering of a porcelain plate on the wall. As my mother and father argued, the commentator's voice continued to crackle throughout the kitchen.

"We see the time remaining in the seventh round... not much..."

"Those sheets feel *warm*!" my father shouted, spit flying everywhere. "Warm when I haven't touched them in hours!"

"Oh, Jesus Christ, Paul, there's nothing inside that thick head of yours but suspicion! It's driving me goddamn crazy!"

Another plate shattered across the floor.

"God dammit! Is there anything in yours at all?!"

"This isn't about me! When was the last time you made a goddamn sale, Paul? When was the last time you brought... brought home some *good* news about—"

The commentator's voice continued to blare. *"Looks like it could be ending here in the seventh—"*

And that's when I saw it reflected in the screen of the television.

Behind me, framed in the doorway of the kitchen, I saw my father strike my mother across the face. She stumbled backward and into the open dishwasher. Dozens of plates shattered beneath her as she cried out.

And as I ran up the stairs, I heard the commentator's voice laughing as he shouted, *"And with that left hook, it's all over! All over folks! A knockout right there! It's all over!"*

* * * * *

Have you ever been sent to the corner store to get powder for your mother's black eye?

The only sound in there was the humming of the two slushy machines-- both red. I walked to the back of the store, where several small pans of makeup were stacked beside a few boxes of condoms and fake eyelashes.

With the small pan in my hand, I hurried toward the counter, embarrassed that somebody would see me buying makeup.

"Good evening, sir," the cashier said glumly, popping several bubbles of her gum on the roof of her mouth. "Did you find everything you were looking for today?"

"Yes. Thank you."

She punched several buttons on the register.

"You do realize this is makeup, right, sir?"

"Yes. Thank you."

"That'll be three dollars and sixty eight cents, sir."

I thrust a ten into her manicured fingers. She dumped the change into my hand and said, "Thank you. Have a nice day."

I hurried out the door, which chimed behind me. I propped up my bike again, which I'd rested against the concrete wall, right beneath the letters of "CORNER CARE CONVENIENCE STORE."

And as I rode off, back toward my house, I couldn't really explain what I was feeling. You can't explain moments like that, but they do things to you, you know? You never forget moments like that, as long as you live.

I came to a sudden halt and let my bike fall. I just stared for several long moments at the silent face of Brendan's house. I saw movement in one of the upstairs windows. A black silhouette was moving back and forth inside the room as yellow light spilled out of the window and slanted across the roof shingles.

And in that moment, I realized what was so sad about the whole thing. I knew that nothing would ever fix all of the bad moments, because they'd never go away. Moments like this could never be fixed. I knew that.

But you know what? They could have been made better. Moments like this wouldn't have been so hard if the people who loved you kept their promises.

He didn't keep his, did he? Not too long ago, we'd wrapped our pinkies around each other's and promised to always be children. His eyes still sparkled that day, but they don't sparkle the same way anymore.

What happened? Who took Brendan away from me?

That night, I lied in bed and stared up at the ceiling. At one point, I heard crying from outside of my window. When I looked out, onto the street, I saw a few neighborhood boys hurrying home while nursing red hands.

I tried to sleep, but for some reason, it wouldn't come. All night, I could hear my mother wandering up and down the hallway outside of my room, talking to the portraits on the wall like they were people. Every few minutes, she'd hiccup and then cry for a few seconds before falling silent and passing out while leaning against the wall.

It's sad because my Mom used to be such a beautiful woman. If you would look at the old photographs, you'd see it. She used to have a light in her eyes, and maybe those days are gone now, but they still feel close. I wish I could find the words to tell her now that I'll always love her. I wish I could somehow reach her, but I knew the harder I'd try, the less she'd hear me.

I've said quite a few bad things about her in this story, but she really was beautiful. I know it's awfully strange that I'm saying this, but this story is coming to its close and I think it's important that you know that she used to kiss my cuts when I was younger after I'd fall off of my bicycle.

My mother wasn't a bad person, okay? She was part of my childhood— some of the best parts, and I can never thank her enough for that.

As the night drew on and I became so immune to the ticking of the clock that I barely heard it anymore, my mother's whispers and light footsteps finally stopped. The entire house was quiet. Everybody was asleep— everybody except for me.

Then, I had an idea.

"Mom?" I whispered, pushing my bedroom door open and peeking through the crack.

She didn't answer me, so I knew she wasn't awake. I crept out into the hallway, grabbed her half-empty bottle of wine and retreated back to my room where I pushed the door closed and took several deep gulps before gagging and crouching over the floor because I thought I was going to vomit.

The wine was sweet— but the aftertaste was a lot like vinegar. I collapsed onto my bed, pinched my nose and choked down a couple more swigs and then sat there and waited for something— *anything*— to happen. As I sat there, I became aware of the ticking of the clock again— which had grown painfully loud. Over the next hour, the more I drank, the slower time seemed to pass, until I wasn't sure if it was passing at all anymore.

"Tommy?" I whispered, groggily. "Come out."

Silence. I squeezed my eyes closed and prayed for sleep. When I'd been lying awake until nearly half past two, I opened my eyes. Since I was so dizzy, the roses on the wallpaper seemed to dance.

"Tommy, come out!" I demanded. I rose from my bed and stumbled over to my closet. I pulled open the doors and scowled because my closet was empty, apart from several rattling hangers. Next, I stumbled toward my window and yanked it open.

"Tommy!" I called out of the window. "Can you hear me?!"

But again, nothing.

He wasn't outside. He wasn't under my bed. He wasn't *anywhere*.

Where were you, Tommy? What were you doing that night?

I swallowed a few more gulps of wine before curling up on the floor at the foot of my bed. Even though I was dizzy and it was dark, I could still make out the outline of the dresser that had my rocket ship pajamas inside. As my eyes traveled down the closed drawers, I grew

134

angry. I leapt across the room and pulled open my dresser. I wasn't sure where the anger came from, but I yanked open the drawer that had Brendan's birthday card inside. I grabbed hold of it and spat on it before I tore it to pieces.

I threw the pieces through my bedroom window. The bits of paper twirled and danced in the air for several moments until a gust of wind carried them away like lost flower petals.

I regretted tearing up Brendan's card the moment that I'd done it. Angry with myself, I kicked at the wall with my bare foot and then hissed in pain because my toe started bleeding beneath the nail. Afterward, I fell back into my bed and squeezed my eyes shut.

"Please, Tommy," I begged. "*Please come out.*"

And in that moment, I had another idea.

I gently opened my bedroom door and tip-toed out into the hallway. My mother's face was pressed against the wall. She was snoring loudly and the thick powder that had been covering her black eye had rubbed off against the wallpaper.

I kissed her on the forehead before hurrying past her, down the stairs and out the front door. I ran across the street to the playground, which was lit with those terrible, orange street lights.

It wasn't long before I was pushing my way through the leaves and branches of one of the bushes— the one where I had seen Harold Stacy lying inside three years before. Remember that day? The day he asked me to pretend that I never saw him and it was the last time I ever spoke to him before they took him away from us?

Once inside the cover of the leaves, I stared up at the sky through the branches and even though I was all alone, I felt safer than I had in months.

I curled up into a tight ball to keep myself warm because I wasn't wearing my rocket ship pajamas. The world was spinning around me, and I could feel the vein in my temple pulsating, but I still managed to fall asleep because I felt like I was in the company of an old friend.

At first, my dreams were blurry and dark. I couldn't make sense of any of them because they were just bits of old memories. While I watched them flicker before my eyes, I chewed down on my lips until the bottom one cracked open and I could taste blood. Eventually, all the haze settled and I felt awfully lonely because there was only darkness in my dreams that night and for whatever reason, I wanted to kill myself again as I stared into it. I'm sure many people wouldn't understand why and that's okay. It's not that I wanted to die. I just didn't want to live, either. I didn't want anything at all— only Tommy Swanson.

"Tommy?" I called through the darkness.

But there was no response. For a moment or two, I fumbled forward until, all at once, I woke up. I could see the sky through the break in the branches again. When the world around me began to spin, I cried out in fright and leaned over to vomit.

"Tommy?" I managed to choke out. "Why aren't you here?"

I knew the answer even before I finished asking. He wasn't there because I wasn't dreaming.

"Where are you?" I cried, nearly out of breath. "I need you!"

I could smell my vomit now— and that made me feel ill again. When I looked down at it, I felt terribly guilty because I had ruined the place that used to be Harold Stacy's favorite spot to watch the stars.

I crawled my way out of the bushes before I had the opportunity to get sick again. As I stumbled across the basketball court on my way to the playground, I had to steady myself a few times so I wouldn't fall and hit my head.

Once on the playground, I collapsed onto one of the swings. I tried to keep as still as possible so that I wouldn't get sick again. I could still taste my vomit and smell it on my feet because I'd stepped in it on my way out of the bushes.

The smell was awful— just like the spoiled milk inside the milk carton that had Susan Smith's missing photograph on the back of it. The smell reminded me of the time my mother had gotten sick all over the sofa a few weeks earlier and I had to clean it up because I knew my father was going to yell at her if he found it, and I didn't want him to yell at her anymore because that'd just make her drink more.

As I sat there on those swings, I stared at the sky and wondered if heaven was going to be a place where Brendan and I were still young and my mother smelled like perfume instead of brandy and Brendan's father didn't bleed when he coughed and Susan Smith would be dancing in a field instead of dying in one. I pictured heaven to be full of buildings that were tall and green— just like Emerald City in the unedited reels of *The Wizard of Oz*. I imagined heaven to feel free— just like the breeze atop the Ferris wheel on summer nights.

Suddenly, I had a terrible idea that scared me and excited me at the same time. At first, I tried to push the idea out of my head, but the more I tried, the more wonderful it sounded.

In that moment, I made a promise to myself. I promised that I was going to buy one last ticket to the carnival. I was going to ride the Ferris wheel without Brendan for the first time in my life. Normally, the thought of that made me sad because I'd have nobody to kiss when the Ferris Wheel stopped at the top, but this time would be different because I wouldn't need anybody to kiss at the top because I was going to jump instead.

I'm going to die, I thought to myself, and for whatever reason, I started laughing. I don't know why I couldn't stop, but I just laughed until I cried and I'll never know why I did that.

Maybe it's because I was excited. In my mind, heaven was a place that was filled with sprinklers that never ran dry and big backyards and cloudless skies and mothers who cleaned your cuts instead of drunken mothers who needed to be cleaned up after.

But I was afraid— and I'm not ashamed to admit it. I was nervous that when I hit the ground, I'd be all alone and heaven would be a place without anybody or anything.

As I stared up at the night sky, I had another idea. It was a terrible idea because I needed six stitches before morning, but I did it anyway. With shaky legs, I crept back across the street. The front door to my house was open because I'd forgotten to close it, so I slipped inside without a sound. My mother had left the television on inside of the den. I could see a beautiful woman holding a box of Betty Crocker cake mix and smiling.

"The perfect cake, each and every time!"

I grabbed hold of the phone and made a quick telephone call before creeping back outside and into the night. The mulch crunched beneath my bare feet as I started to climb up the wrong end of the slide. Once I made it to the top, I sat inside the fort where I'd once given Brendan his birthday present. Afterward, I climbed my way to the plastic roof of the fort and laid down across it.

The wind felt wonderful up there. From where I sat, the sky felt close, and even though I was so dizzy, the stars didn't move at all. They twinkled and I tried to grab hold of them like fireflies.

"Tommy," I whispered one last time. "Are you here?"

When nobody answered me, I rose to my feet. My legs were wobbly because of the wine, or maybe it was because I was afraid of the pain. Regardless, I turned my back to the hopscotch squares on the sidewalk, closed my eyes and stepped backward.

I fell. As I did, I felt like I was *flying*. My lips broke into a smile and I laughed and cried at the same time and then...

SMACK!

My back landed on the mulch, but my head hit the edge of the sidewalk. My body didn't even have time to register any pain. Everything immediately went black and the playground around me vanished. The mulch was gone. The stars disappeared. The sticky summer air became crips and cold. For what felt like hours, I floated around in darkness and I couldn't help but laugh because it felt like I was still *falling.*

Suddenly, I felt my arms and fingertips brushing against something cold. *The mulch,* I realized, and I became grounded again.

When I opened my eyes, I saw the stars, but they were falling all around me like rain. I tried to move my hands because I wanted to catch them, but I couldn't move at all, so I smiled and just watched. The falling stars were so beautiful and for a moment, I thought that I was in heaven.

Then, I saw him. He was blurry at first, but it wasn't long before he came into focus.

Tommy Swanson was crying. His lips were moving frantically and he kept shaking me, but I couldn't hear what he was saying because the only sound that I could hear was a deep hum. I wasn't sure where it was coming from, but after several moments, I realized that it was coming from inside of my head. It was quiet at first, but the longer it continued, the higher it rose until it was so loud that my head felt close to bursting.

Then, I saw the moon. It was so bright that night. Its light fell across Tommy's bare chest. It was the most beautiful thing I'd ever seen.

"Let's go to the moon," I whispered with a laugh. "Tommy, let's go to the *moon* one day."

I could feel a few of Tommy's tears on my face. I could hear him now— faintly. He was shouting my name, but his voice sounded so far away.

"Tommy," I breathed, reaching out my hand until I could press it against his rosy cheeks. "You're *here.*"

"Christ, kid," he cried, grabbing hold of my hand. His felt sticky and wet...

"Tommy, why are your hands...?"

"There's so much *blood…*" he cried. "It's *everywhere*."

"I'm sorry, Tommy. I didn't mean to make such a mess."

"Christ, Hunter!" he shouted, squeezing my hand. "What did you *do*?!"

"Am I dying?"

He didn't answer me. Instead, he tried scooping up the blood that had already drained from the crack in the back of my head.

"Tell me," I pleaded, my voice straining. "Am I *dying*?"

"You're not gonna die!" he said frantically. "Not like this."

"It'll be okay, Tommy."

"No!" he hollered, his eyes wild. "You're not gonna die! Don't say that!"

"Tommy, please…"

"HELP!" Tommy shouted, turning toward the line of houses across the street. "SOMEBODY, HELP!"

"Tommy…"

"GODDAMMIT IT! SOMEBODY HELP!"

"There isn't time—"

"You can't die! Not here! You're all alone! Christ, you can't die all *alone*!"

Alone. The word echoed throughout the night. I grabbed hold of his arm and squeezed it as hard as I could. His eyes met mine, and when they did, I smiled.

"What the hell are you smiling about?!" he demanded, more tears rolling down his cheeks.

"I'm not alone," I whispered. "I'm with you."

When I said that, his lips broke into a pained smile. He laughed through a few more tears and squeezed my hand so tightly that I could barely feel it anymore.

Then suddenly, I could hear sirens. Tommy's eyes grew wide because he heard them, too.

"Sirens!" he exclaimed. "You hear that, Hunter? They're coming. Somebody must've just called them." Afterward, he turned toward them and waved his hands through the air. "OVER HERE! YOU HEAR ME?! HE'S OVER HERE!"

My eyes fluttered and I managed to whisper, "I was the one who called."

Tommy stopped waving his hands and turned back toward me. "*You* did?"

"I can't die tonight."

His brow furrowed. Suddenly, there was anger. "You jumped off the goddamn swing set like a madman! There's so much *blood*! What the hell were you thinking?!"

"I wanted to see you."

"Christ, kid! I'm here! I've always been here. You didn't need to do *this*."

"Please," I begged, my voice growing weaker. "I need you to promise me something before I go."

All at once, his anger vanished. He leaned in a bit and his face grew blue because he seemed to forget to breathe. "Anything."

The sound of the sirens drew closer.

"Ride the Ferris wheel with me tomorrow and when we stop at the top... I'm too afraid to do it alone. I just... I need you to hold my hand while we... while we..."

My voice faded to silence and I started to cry. I didn't need to finish because Tommy knew what I was going to say. Suddenly, I was embarrassed by how weak I was. I was embarrassed that I was afraid to die alone and needed him to hold my hand.

"You want me to...?"

"Tommy, promise me."

"Hunter, I..."

"Promise me!" I shouted, my vision growing darker. "We're running out of time! I need this!"

"You're not thinking straight!"

"I've found the way to make childhood last forever! It's here! With you!"

And that's when I grabbed hold of his hand. I held it as tightly as I could and when I finally released it, I outstretched my pinky. Several moments passed when we just stared into each other's eyes. Then, all at once, he kissed me. He kissed me and for the first time in awhile, I felt fireworks inside of me. Then, after the kiss, I felt him close his pinky around mine.

"I promise," he whispered.

Suddenly, I heard talking. I felt hands on my body. Somebody grabbed hold of my wrist.

"He's still alive," I heard a voice say.

"We need a stretcher!" called another.

I winced when one of them touched the back of my head.

"BE CAREFUL!" Tommy roared as the figure kept touching my head.

"He's lost blood."

"He'll need some stitches."

"CHRIST, BE CAREFUL!" Tommy pleaded again. "You're hurting him!"

I felt my body being lifted. I tried to smile to Tommy, to let him know that I'd be okay, but I suddenly felt terribly dizzy and the world around me started to vanish into wisps of smoke. I couldn't see the playground anymore. I couldn't see the figures or the ambulance. I couldn't even see the moon.

But I could still see Tommy Swanson, who watched them carry me away. His pinky was still outstretched, exactly where it had been when he'd wrapped it around mine. His hand looked lonely and cold and I wished I could hold it again.

Then, he was gone. The smoke overtook him and I couldn't see or feel anything anymore.

The Night I Returned To The Carnival

Brendan,

    I've known for awhile now that I'm in love with you— ever since we wrapped our pinkies around one another's at the carnival. I know it's not your birthday today, so you won't be expecting a card in your mailbox, but I just wanted to say a few things, okay? First, I want you to know that you'll be very happy one day. I know you will. Second, I don't want you to miss me because I'll be here. I'll be in your dreams somewhere. That's a place where nobody will see us— your dreams. It took me awhile to realize that. I don't want you to ever feel guilty about what you dream about, okay?

And finally, you may not believe it, but I'll be waiting for you. You won't be able to see me— but I'll be there. I'll be at the top of the Ferris wheel every single year, waiting. And if you feel something when you're up there, don't be afraid. It'll be me holding your hand. Just remember that, okay? Remember that and things will never have to change.

    Thank you for giving me the best childhood I could ever ask for.

        Love, Hunter

* * * * *

I slid the note inside Brendan's mailbox the following evening. For several moments, I just stood at the end of Brendan's driveway, staring up at the light coming from inside Brendan's bedroom window.

I wrote the letter on a hospital napkin that they'd given me beside some meatloaf and bright red gelatin. I needed seven stitches in the back of my head. They still itched and stung several hours afterward, but the doctor sent me home with some Oxycontin and that made them feel better. By midday, half of the bottle was missing and nobody said anything to my mom even though we knew she'd put them somewhere.

The entire day had been terribly strange— from my father's reaction to my mother's apathy. My father thought it'd been an accident and my mother didn't really think about it at all. He was mad that I'd been drinking and my mother tried to be, but deep down, she knew she couldn't be because my father would just blame her and that would make everything worse.

I watched the sunrise from my hospital bed because I thought I should see it one final time. It's interesting how colors look brighter when you think you're going to die. You notice details in things that you'd never cared to pay attention to before— like the way the underside of the leaves look in the wind and the way little pieces of the sidewalk sparkle in the morning sun.

I wrote out my note to Brendan and when I left the hospital, I tucked it inside my pocket. The entire family spent the rest of the day in the den, and when Jamie went into the backyard to play and my mother called Mrs. Samuelson on the phone and my dad went into the kitchen to get me some ice cream, I slid out the front door, ran across the neighborhood, and pushed the note into Brendan's mailbox.

My mother was watching the Wizard of Oz in the kitchen when I returned home from Brendan's. A half-melted ice cream sundae was sitting beside her on the kitchen table. She had a large chicken pot pie and peas in front of her, but it wasn't even steaming because she was too busy giggling into her glass of wine.

I wondered what she was going to say when I was gone. I hoped something good would come out of it— maybe she'd stop drinking. Maybe she'd cry and hug Jamie and realize that memories were too precious.

As I thought about that, I sat down beside her. I knew that she wouldn't remember any of it, but for whatever reason, I knew that spending time with her was the right thing to do.

To be honest, and I know this sounds terribly selfish, but for whatever reason, I was hoping that, somehow, she'd look at me and say something— *anything*, that would make me decide to stay.

It was terribly ironic, but in that moment, the Wicked Witch appeared on the television screen and turned over an hourglass. Red sand began to pour into the bottom and she screeched, "You see that? That's how much longer you've got to be alive!"

My mother took another long sip of wine. "I was the witch once for Halloween, back when I was just a little girl. It's funny, isn't it? How you can remember the strangest things?"

She rose from her seat and emptied her full plate into the garbage disposal. The loud hum made me cringe. Afterward, she drifted over to the refrigerator and refilled her wine glass.

"Yeah, it's funny," I whispered, not sure what to say.

"Oh, I probably have old photos somewhere! I wonder where those have gone…"

I didn't say anything. Instead, I nearly leapt out of my seat because the cuckoo clock on the wall burst to life and the cardinal cried out.

My mom returned to the table. On the television, Dorothy was shouting, "*I'm frightened Auntie Em! I'm frightened!*"

My mother leaned toward me and I instinctually backed away because I knew that smelling the alcohol on her breath would make me feel worse.

"I had the best witch laugh. All of the other girls wondered how I did it…"

Suddenly, she fell silent and her facial expression changed. She no longer giggled into her wine, but instead, stared up at the ceiling with eyes wider than dinner plates.

"That was so long ago. I was just a little girl, but I remember it so vividly. My mother and father…. they needed to take me to so many shops that day because… well, because…"

My gaze traveled away from the television, which was now lit with detergent and auto-repair commercials.

My mother laughed in disbelief. Her eyes danced across the empty ceiling, but I could tell that her memories were playing across her eyes like an old movie. "Because…. oh my… it couldn't have been… I remember it now. All of the stores were sold out of *green* face paint. We had to go to nearly ten different places before we found some! This was before Barnaby's ever came to town at all, when I was just a little girl. When things were so… *different*."

She placed a hand over the top of her heart.

"I feel so strange now. Oh, why do I feel this way? I'd just forgotten… that's all. It's been so terribly long since then. The stores don't sell green face paint anymore, do they? That's quite sad, don't you think? What if a little girl wants to be a witch for Halloween? What do we do then?"

I stood up from my seat.

"Where are you going?" she asked, pulled from her daydream.

"The carnival," I told her for the fourth time that evening.

"That's where I met your father," she said with a smile. "Did I ever tell you that story? He was trying to win me a stuffed bear and I—"

"Ended up winning one for him," I finished as I pushed in my chair and headed toward the front door.

"Don't forget your keys!" she exclaimed.

I turned, and when I did, I saw her pointing to where I'd left them on the kitchen table.

147

"Thanks," I mumbled, snatching them up and then hurrying down the hall toward the front door. Before I could reach it, I heard the thundering of footsteps on the stairs and quickly tried to leave before Jamie could stop me.

"Hunter?!" he called, excitedly.

I was just about to close the door when he grabbed hold of it.

"Are you going to the carnival?"

"Yeah," I said, my mouth dry. "But I'm late. I have to go."

"Do you think I could come along, too?"

There was a light of hope in his eyes and I felt terribly guilty for squashing it.

"Maybe some other time. I'm meeting some friends."

"Oh, come on!" he said, grabbing my arm. "I'll be cool, I promise."

"Jamie, not tonight."

"I could win you and your friends candy! All those games are rigged, but I know how to beat them!"

"Go back upstairs," I said, "I'll take you to the carnival tomorrow."

The lie stung as it left my lips. Jamie smiled and his eyes twinkled.

"Just you and me?"

I sighed. "Just you and me."

And then I hurried down the front steps, leaving Jamie standing in the open doorway with a smile that killed me. I could feel his eyes watching me as I went, and suddenly, I started to cry. He couldn't hear me, since I was so far away, but all at once, I stopped walking.

"Jamie?" I said, turning around again.

Jamie didn't answer, but I knew he was listening. I kept my eyes rooted on the ground because I didn't want him to see me crying and I knew that if I looked into his eyes again, I would stay.

"Goodbye," I whispered so low that he couldn't even hear.

"What did you say?"

"I said *goodbye*!" I stammered angrily, even though I didn't mean to.

And the tears came harder. I tried to wipe them away before Jamie could notice, but the harder I tried, the more obvious they became.

"Hunter... why are you—"

"*GOODBYE*!" I shouted one final time, my voice cracking, before turning and sprinting across the remainder of the front lawn. I ran so fast away from that house that I nearly tripped a few times because my feet couldn't keep up with my legs.

* * * * *

I stopped running when I could see the lights of the carnival in the distance. For a few moments, I tried to steady my spinning head. The pills were wearing off and I could feel the back of my head beginning to throb again.

The golden gates to Barnaby's Traveling Carnival were just as foreboding as they were when I was thirteen-years-old. I paid a quarter to the woman at the entrance just like I'd done the night my childhood ended.

The crowded carnival pathways were littered with hamburger wrappers and soggy tickets. All of the children had lights in their eyes and red balloons tied around their wrists. I heard a distant lion's roar and the faint echo of applause. An announcer, the same as before, was standing atop a barrel and smacking his cane against a sign that read, "ELEPHANT SLAUGHTERING TICKETS."

He chewed on his toothpick and shouted, "The next show will be starting in 15 minutes, folks! I repeat, 15 minutes!"

When my eyes traveled to the tent behind him, a moldy sign read, "SLAUGHTERING ENTRANCE." Beneath it, several children were exiting. They laughed and rubbed the elephant blood from their eyes. Behind them, their fathers slicked back their hair with it.

A short walk later, I was standing under the Ferris wheel and staring up at the top gondola. Two figures were inside of it, but I couldn't distinguish their faces. I wondered who they were and what their childhood was like.

The line was long. A clown was weaving between the line on a unicycle and tying balloons to everyone's wrists. A shiver crawled down my spine when I saw him because I recognized his fat thighs and toothy grin.

He was the clown that kept staring at me after Brendan left me behind on the Ferris wheel. Do you remember that clown? The one that had the half-moon painted on his left cheek?

When he got to me, I kept my head down because I didn't want him to recognize me. I could hear his rough breathing and feel it against my neck as he tied a balloon around my wrist. When he was done, I started losing circulation in my hand because he tied it too tightly. He then pulled two long balloons from his pocket and tied them into swords for the boys in front of me to play with.

They jabbed one another with them and rolled around in the grass and laughed.

As they pretended to die, I became nervous and frightened. I felt alone in that moment, so I closed my eyes and whispered, "Are you here?"

It was so quiet that nobody in line could hear.

"Show me."

POP! The balloon that had been tied to my wrist suddenly burst. There were several more pops and I watched as the children's balloons that were shaped like daggers popped, too. All of the children leapt back in shock and one of them even cried.

"*Tommy,*" I whispered, but as his name left my lips, I saw that the clown was watching me now. I wanted to scream when our eyes met because his hair was so greasy and his smile was so chapped and wide and it reminded me of every nightmare I'd ever had since I was young.

I shot my gaze back down to the grass and I prayed that he would ride away on his unicycle and I'd never have to stare into his empty eyes again, but when I looked up again, he was closer— so close that when he laughed, the spit from his lips landed on the side of my face.

That's when he grabbed hold of my shirt. At first, I tried to pull his hands off of me because he was pulling on my collar so hard that it was beginning to choke me. His grasp was too strong, so I started swinging at him. All the while, the children and crowd around me began to laugh and point and cheer like it was a show.

When I finally managed to wrangle free, the clown stumbled backward. He let out one final laugh, right in my face, and his breath smelled like fruit that had gone bad. Several silent moments crawled by, and before I could say anything to the clown at all, he smiled a terrible smile and vanished into the darkness behind one of the tents.

I was terrified of where the clown was going. Did he see something the night that I tried to kiss Brendan atop the Ferris wheel? Did he know that I was... *different*?

And if he had seen something, who was he going to tell?

The Night Another Neighborhood Boy Died

I didn't want to hurt anybody else that night. I promise that if I had known what was about to happen, I wouldn't have gotten onto the Ferris wheel. I would've ran back home to the playground because nobody else in this story deserved to die.

But I was selfish and I have to try to forgive myself.

About twenty-five minutes after that clown disappeared, I was slowly inching my way to the front of the line of the Ferris wheel. Meanwhile, Brendan was at home flicking through the television channels until he stopped on one that was playing Mickey Mouse cartoons. Brendan always liked Mickey Mouse. Sometimes, when I was younger, I'd try to mimic Mickey's voice to make Brendan laugh. He always would and it would make me feel really warm.

That night, Brendan said he was trying really hard to find something to make him laugh. When Mickey Mouse couldn't do it, he was just about to change the channel when he heard a loud crash from the front yard. It was followed by a scream, one that made Brendan afraid. He hurried to the front door and pulled it open to see Gabriel leaping out of a car. Beside it, Brendan's mailbox was laying on the ground. The red flag was snapped and the wooden pole that held the mailbox was splintered and broken.

"Goddammit!" Gabriel shouted, running his hands through his hair and kicking at the tire of his car.

"What happened?" Brendan asked, hurrying down the porch stairs and across the front lawn.

Suddenly, Gabriel's eyes grew wide. "Don't tell Mom. It was an accident, ya hear?"

"You're not hurt, are you?"

"I'm fine. I just…. I *saw somebody.*"

Brendan's eyes narrowed. "Who?"

"I saw a.... a...." Gabriel's voice faded to silence as he whirled around, searching the darkness around him. "He was just standing in the driveway and I nearly goddamn hit him!"

"What did he look like?"

"It was so dark! I needed to swerve at the last minute!"

Brendan furrowed his brow. Gabriel's eyes didn't look the way they usually did. They weren't a chestnut brown, more of a black, and the whites were bloodshot and full of veins that looked thicker than before.

"You're not... seeing things again, are you?"

"I'm not *seeing things*," Gabriel protested hotly. He puffed out his chest and jabbed his finger into Brendan's chest.

Brendan backed away, clenching his teeth because Gabriel's finger had pressed hard against the tender spot beneath his sternum. He was about to apologize when, all of a sudden, Gabriel leapt backward and pointed wildly across the street toward their neighbor's lawn.

"There he is again! Do you see him?!"

Brendan looked, but he didn't see anything and turned back to Gabriel, worried.

"What's the matter with you?"

Gabriel wiped his sweating forehead before whispering, "Is Mom inside?"

"No. She's at the Carmichaels' dinner party— where *you*'re supposed to be."

Gabriel ran his hands through his hair, suddenly more tense than before. He pulled a few things from his pockets and shoved them into Brendan's hands.

"Hide these for me, okay? I need you to do this. She could be home any minute now and... hell, she's gonna know..."

Brendan looked down at his hands, which now contained a lighter and a small bag of something *green*.

"What... is this?"

"Just take it and hide it, okay? She won't snoot around in your room!"

Brendan's eyes narrowed as he stared into Gabriel's bloodshot ones. "Gabriel, are you...?"

Suddenly, Gabriel leapt backward like a frightened cat. "I see him again!" he cried. "DO YOU SEE HIM?!"

Brendan spun around, and when he did, that's when he saw the clown watching them through the leaves of the neighbor's bushes. The powdered face and crooked smile seemed to float in darkness. Even from fifty feet away, Brendan could make out a blue crescent moon beneath the clown's left eye.

"DO YOU SEE IT?!" Gabriel roared again, grabbing hold of Brendan by the shoulder.

"I.. I *do*..." Brendan choked out.

Brendan couldn't really remember many details about what happened next— but he told me that Gabriel yanked open the car door and pulled something small and black from the glove box. The sound of several bullets blasted throughout the night and Brendan wrestled a gun from Gabriel's hand.

"Gabriel!"

"DO YOU SEE HIM?!"

"Gabriel, stop!"

"I see him— everywhere I go! He's always there!"

When Brendan shot another glance toward the neighbor's bushes, the clown had vanished. For a moment or two, Brendan tried to keep Gabriel calm even though he wasn't calm, himself. Before he could stop Gabriel, he had hopped back inside of his car and sped down the street, leaving Brendan cradling the gun alone.

Brendan turned back to where he'd last seen the clown. The wind was blowing the branches of all the bushes and Brendan couldn't tell if any of them were moving because of the clown hiding inside of them. He raised the gun with trembling hands. "Stay back!" he called. "Don't come any closer!"

A sickening laugh greeted him from somewhere in the darkness. When Brendan heard it, he said a cold sweat broke out across his forehead and he hurried back inside his house and locked the front door behind him. In the den, he could hear the ghostly and melodic voices of several late night performers on the television. The light from the television poured out into the hallway and glistened across the black and white photographs of his father that hung on the wall.

As he hurried down the hallway, he almost dropped the gun a few times because his hands were sweating so badly. Once inside the den, he raced to turn on all of the lights because he was afraid of the darkness. Before he could, he cried out because he saw the shadowy silhouette of the clown passing by the windows.

He tightened his grip on the gun.

"What do you want?!" Brendan shouted, raising it again.

Thump! Thump! Thump! The clown began pounding on the glass.

"I'm warning you!" Brendan hollered. "I'll... I'll shoot!"

Then suddenly, there was silence. The silhouette vanished. All Brendan could hear now was laughter from the television.

The room was still dark. Brendan turned on the lamps beside the sofa and then backed up against the wall so he could watch the windows. He told me that it felt like he was staring at them for hours, even though it couldn't have been more than a few minutes.

Beside him, the television kept flashing to cutaways of American sailors, factory workers and children eating hamburgers.

155

"And as all of you are certainly aware," the television host said, *"Today marks twenty years since the United States detonated the atomic bomb code-named "Slappy" over the Soviet Union..."*

Suddenly, the television switched to a cutaway of a large mushroom cloud. As it did, Brendan heard a loud crash, and at first, he thought it was coming from the television, but he realized a patio chair had been thrown through the window of the den. It tumbled across the carpet before colliding with the television. One of the legs pierced the screen and there was a flash of electricity before the lights flickered to darkness.

Brendan told me he didn't even scream because he didn't have time to. He just fired the gun. He fired three times at the clown who had started climbing through the broken window. At first, Brendan thought he missed. Moments later, Brendan could see the blood. One of the bullets had hit the clown's shoulder. The other had hit his navel.

Stunned at what he'd done, Brendan fell to his knees and began to cry. "HELP!" he shouted. "SOMEBODY HELP ME!"

When nobody came, Brendan cried harder. He told me that he shouted for Gabriel and then he shouted for his mother. When they didn't come, Brendan said he shouted for a third person.

He never told me who that third person was.

At first, I thought he shouted for me, but the more I think about it, the more I think that he shouted for his dad.

* * * * *

I heard the gunshots from the line to the Ferris wheel, but I didn't know they were gunshots at the time. I could barely hear them over the laughing children and lion roars. Moments later, a flock of birds flew overhead. I wondered where they were going and what it felt like to fly.

Would I be flying away that night, too? When people die, do they finally fly?

When my gaze returned from the sky, I noticed that somebody was waving to me. At first, I couldn't make out his face because he was too far away. He kept jumping up and down, waving his hands around in the air.

"Hunter!" he called. I couldn't hear him well, but I could read his lips.

When I realized who it was, I waved back.

Do you remember the boy whose ball got caught in the tree the day that my childhood ended? His name was Simon. He lived three houses down from me. Before I slid my note in Brendan's mailbox, I went to Simon's house. There were balloons in the hallway behind him when he answered the door. He had just turned nine a few days earlier.

"Hello," I said when his curious eyes met mine. "I'm Hunter. Do you remember me?"

He quickly nodded. "You're one of the older boys."

I smiled. "You just turned nine this year, huh?" .

He nodded again, this time more forceful.

"Wow. You're getting older. A little bit taller, too. Say, how about you do me a favor?"

"What is it?"

I pulled a stack of envelopes from my pocket. "These are for my friend. He lives in the house with the green grass. His name's Brendan."

Simon took the envelopes and examined them. "I know where that is. What's inside of them?"

"Birthday cards. I've always given him a card on his birthday. I think it makes him happy."

Simon was about to open one, but I grabbed hold of his hand before he could.

"You can't open them," I laughed. "I need somebody to put one of them in his mailbox every year. I have the dates on the front. Do you think you could do that? It's really important. I'm sure he'd be sad without them."

Simon shuffled through them. "Why don't you just do it?"

"Because I'm moving away."

His face fell. "Moving away?"

"Don't worry. I won't be too far."

"Will you come visit?"

I was about to tell him that I wasn't, but before I could, his eyes met mine again. I'm not sure why, but he reminded me of myself in that moment. He had a curiosity like I always had and the way he talked sounded a lot like Brendan.

So as I stared back at him, I whispered, "I'm not sure," because I had no way of knowing if Simon would dream about me at night the way I dreamt about Tommy Swanson.

"I got an envelope here for you, too," I told him, pulling one final envelope from my pocket. "Open it on your thirteenth birthday. Not a day before. Do you understand?"

He snatched it from my hands and held it up to the light in hopes that he'd be able to see what was inside.

"When I'm thirteen? That feels like forever."

"It'll come sooner than you think. So, do we have a deal?"

When I outstretched my hand, he shook it.

"I'm counting on you," I said. "Bye, Simon."

And then, I turned away. I heard him close the front door behind me. When I looked back over my shoulder, I could see him through the window, hurrying up the stairs toward his room. The envelopes were cradled tightly to his chest.

I smiled as he disappeared from view. I didn't know Simon that well, but just from our brief encounters, I knew that there was something strange about him. That's why I gave him the cards, especially the one for him. Inside, I wrote out a note. It wasn't too long or anything. It was pretty short, actually. To be entirely honest, I knew that he may never read it or even need to. He may forget about it and turn thirteen and throw stones at the boys and girls inside the freak tent and grow up to drink too much whiskey like all the other men.

But maybe he wouldn't.

Maybe he'd keep the envelope safe and hide it in his drawer beneath his pajamas the way I hid the birthday cards that Brendan had given me. Maybe he'd need it on his thirteenth birthday, the way I needed the cards from Brendan.

It just made me feel better knowing that he had it, you know? Because you can never tell what people will grow up to become and even though I would never know, he had it just in case he grew up to become a boy like me.

* * * * *

I wasn't sure what direction Simon had gone off. The pathways to the carnival were getting crowded because people were beginning to come for the fireworks show.

Only about a dozen people now stood between me and the Ferris wheel. The children in front of me where now playing "I Spy."

"I spy something *red*."

"The balloons?"

"No."

"The tents?"

"No."

Suddenly, we all heard a shout from the front of the line.

"Somebody took it! I took my eyes off of it for *one* goddamn minute!"

It was the ride operator. He was a chunky man with a terrible hairpiece that looked ready to slip off of his shiny head. We all watched him frantically dig through every one of his pockets.

"YOU KIDS!" he bellowed. "WHO TOOK IT?!"

At first, I didn't know who he was talking to. Soon after, my eyes met a group of teenagers who were hanging around the ride exit while laughing and smoking cigarettes. One of the boys, the tallest one, puffed up his chest and snarled, "What did you say?"

I recognized his voice. Michael Evans.

"Who took the key?!" the man shouted. "I can't run the damn ride without it!"

Michael turned back toward his friends, who shrugged even though they had wide smiles across their faces.

"I don't know what you're talking about," Michael said, but I didn't believe him and neither did the operator, who pounded his fist against the operating panel and mumbled something that I didn't hear before getting in Michael's face and demanding he turn out his pockets.

"Somebody took it when I was helping that woman off," he snarled. "You guys have been standing around here since half past nine. You all have this… this *funny* look to you! Like you're up to something!"

"I said we don't know what you're talking about," Michael repeated, this time more firm.

"Then, *turn out your pockets!*"

The man made a grab for Michael's pants, but Michael stepped back. "Who the hell do you think you are? Maybe you should've kept a better eye on it, don't you think?"

As they both argued, I turned my gaze toward the highest gondola, which was gently rocking back and forth. For a second or two, I almost changed my mind. The Ferris wheel looked taller than I remembered, which frightened me, and I wondered whether or not the

Ferris wheel would even be operating since somebody had jacked the key.

Is this a sign? I thought to myself, staring up at the sky. *Should I just go home?*

But the breeze picked up for a moment and wafted the terrible stench of the petting zoo. Beside the petting zoo, I knew the Freak Tent was full of children with bloody thumbs.

"Is the ride going to be working?" one of the little boys in front of me asked his father.

"Of course. Just a bit of a delay."

And as the man ruffled his son's hair, I looked up at the highest gondola again and took a deep breath.

* * * * *

Brendan's voice had finally grown hoarse from shouting so much. The clown, despite having bled all over the carpet, was still breathing. Over the clown's shallow sobs, Brendan could hear his own.

"I'm... *sorry*," he choked out. "I'm so sorry."

He squeezed his eyes shut and raised the gun higher. He was about to pull the trigger again when he heard a terrified cry. When he opened his eyes, he saw that the clown was holding his hands in front of his face. His fingers were chubby and the nails were bitten down so low that they were bleeding.

Before Brendan could say anything, the clown started pulling up the legs of his oversized trousers.

Ivory skin— that's what Brendan saw beneath them. He was shocked because there were veins and blood and everything that makes us *human*.

Soon after, Brendan saw red welts dotting the man's legs like polka dots. At first, Brendan thought the clown was sick. He tried to back further away, but his back was already pressed against the wall.

The clown shouted something incoherent again and that's when Brendan recognized there was... fear.

"Why are you...?"

The clown's eyes started to flutter. His knuckles went white because he was holding onto his trousers so tightly. His body began to tremble, his eyes rolled up in his head, he clenched his mouth closed tightly and arched his back.

That's when Brendan realized the red bumps on the clown's legs weren't bumps at all— they were small carvings. Some were deeper than others. Some had scabbed over and others had scarred completely.

Brendan took several steps forward to get a closer look. As soon as he realized what they were, he let out a cry. As soon as he saw the dozens of rocket ships that the man had carved into his legs, Brendan knew he'd made a terrible mistake.

"Is that you?" he choked out, suddenly falling to the floor beside the clown. "Harold? Harold, is that you?!"

Harold Stacy— the boy who wore rocket ship pajamas the morning that we found Tommy Swanson's body. He vanished from the neighborhood two years later. The rumors were terrible. The older boys said they pulled out his teeth and eyes. Others said they fed him to the lions at the carnival.

But Brendan finally knew the truth. He knew where Harold had been all of those years.

"Harold... what did they *do to you?!*"

Harold tried to speak, but the only thing that came out was a pained laugh and a few droplets of blood.

"Harold, please!"

More laughter. Harold tried to stand, but he had lost too much blood. It was pooling across the carpet and soaking into his trousers.

Brendan grabbed hold of Harold's cheeks and tried to hug his head to his chest. All the while, Harold let out several breathless laughs that sounded like a broken squeaky toy. His breath was warm and foul. Brendan said that it made goosebumps rise all cross his neck.

"Harold, look at me!" Brendan demanded, giving his face several soft slaps. "Don't close your eyes! You hear me?"

But they were already closing, so Brendan tapped him a few times on the side of the face.

"No," Brendan cried. "Keep your eyes open…"

Harold raised a hand and frantically pointed across the room before trying to stand again.

"Harold, you need to stop moving! It's making it worse…"

Harold shook his head. He kept pointing and crying and laughing and that's when Brendan realized that Harold was pointing in the direction of the playground. He didn't know why at the time, but now he understands.

Harold wanted to die on the playground. He wanted Brendan to help him get there so he could crawl into the bush beside the basketball court. That's where he could stare up at the sky through the clearing in the branches and watch the stars while he died.

But Brendan didn't understand, so he kept Harold pinned to the ground while he tried to stop the bleeding, even though he knew that there was nothing that he could do.

And suddenly, Harold became calm and quiet. More tears rolled down Harold's cheeks as he outstretched his body like he was surrounding himself to whatever he saw. He said a few more words that Brendan didn't understand before bursting into laughter.

I'll never know what that laughter sounded like, and I'm afraid that if I did, it'd haunt me for the rest of my life because Brendan said it

sounded like the laughter of a child. Brendan told me that it sounded...
happy. I don't know how Harold was happy, or what he was seeing, but
Brendan said Harold's eyes grew wide, and right before he died, he
looked at Brendan and asked sloppily and slurred, "Are you coming,
too?"

And then his hand went limp, his eyes closed and Harold Stacy
was dead.

The Night Harold Stacy Died

Brendan cried for a long time that night. He didn't even have the television to keep him company while he sat in the den alone— holding Harold Stacy's body in his arms. Once or twice, he could hear the neighborhood boys returning home from the carnival. They laughed and told jokes about the boys and girls of the Freak Tent.

The only time Brendan left Harold's side was to get towels to wipe off all of his clown makeup. Beneath it, Brendan could see scars and acne marks. He wasn't sure the last time that Harold's skin had seen daylight or felt fresh air.

Harold could've been handsome, Brendan thought to himself as he stroked Harold's cheek. Afterward, Brendan sat with Harold and told him stories. He told him all about me and all about his dad. He told Harold about how we missed waving to him when we rode our bicycles around the neighborhood.

Then, something extraordinary happened.

As Brendan sat with Harold, the lights of the house began to flicker. Brendan leapt to his feet, alarmed because he knew that the fuse had blown and he wasn't sure how the lights could be flickering the way that they were.

"Hello…?" he asked, spinning around. "Is somebody here?"

A new sound greeted his ears— one that was coming through the broken window. When Brendan gazed outside, he saw that the sprinkler in the backyard had turned on. It sent water pattering against the back of the house and even through the window.

"HELLO?" Brendan shouted even though nobody was outside to answer. "GABRIEL?"

And that's when Brendan noticed a crumpled up piece of paper stuck in the leaves of one of the bushes. Careful not to cut himself on the glass, Brendan fished it out of the leaves and unfolded it.

It was hard to read at first because the water from the sprinkler had smeared a lot of the writing.

"Dear Brendan," the note started, and Brendan immediately recognized my handwriting.

It was my note— the one that I'd left in Brendan's mailbox. Gabriel had crashed into the mailbox that night and it must've fallen out. Harold must've grabbed it when he crossed Brendan's front yard, but dropped it when Brendan had fired the gun.

"Hunter..." Brendan whispered.

Harold Stacy hadn't come to scare me, Brendan realized. *He'd come to warn me.*

Moments later, Brendan was out the door. His clothing was still covered with Harold's blood, and I'm sure he gave a few of the neighborhood boys a fright as he drove by them on his bicycle. One of them screamed and a few of them started to chase after him because they thought he got in a terrible fight and wanted to ask him about it.

"Hey, wait up!" they called. "You look *bad!* What happened?!"

But Brendan kept riding. As he swept past my house and then the playground, Brendan said that he prayed for his first time outside of church.

He prayed that he was driving in the right direction and maybe there is a God after all, because Brendan was headed straight toward me. He had no way of knowing that at the time. He just peddled— faster and faster, until his legs went numb and his feet blistered inside of his shoes. He rode past Cardinal Street and down the hill toward our school. He rode past the small lake that we all used to visit back when we had a boat before my father sold it to pay for our car.

A few times, the passing cars honked their horns because Brendan was blocking traffic. Once or twice, the cars almost hit Brendan because they must've been distracted by his bloody clothes.

Eventually, Brendan took a shortcut along the creek. It was dark since there were no lights, so Brendan couldn't tell exactly where he was going. He just followed the creek and let the lights of the carnival guide him. Several moments later, he reached a large clearing. In the distance, he could see the lights of the carnival flickering just beyond the tree lining.

"Hunter, just hold on a little longer..."

He prayed again. Then again.

"Hunter, please, I'm almost there..."

Again and again.

His bicycle blasted through the dirt, kicking up a thick cloud in his wake.

Suddenly, he felt a bump beneath his tires and heard what sounded like a crack. He cried out in fright as the bike came crashing to the ground. He hissed in pain because he scraped his elbows on the dirt.

"Damnit..." he spat, grabbing hold of the bike and standing it upright again. He was just about to start riding when he saw what his bike had ridden over— a firework.

The clearing was full of them. For as far as he could see, fireworks were mounted in the dirt and pointed skyward. In the faint moonlight, Brendan could see the two colors— green and red.

"Fireworks..."

Brendan turned toward the Ferris wheel, which wasn't moving anymore. It must've been a quarter mile away, but when Brendan squinted, he could see people shifting around inside the gondolas. He wasn't sure if any of them were me, but he grew frightened when he saw that one of the gondolas only had one person inside of it.

167

He scrambled back onto the bicycle and began peddling, but the chain had broken and he couldn't ride.

"DAMNIT!" he shouted, leaping to the grass and beginning to run.

He weaved between all of the fireworks as fast as he could. While he ran, he felt something weighing down his pockets. He dug his hand inside of them to find the small baggie of green that Gabriel had given him, followed by the zippo lighter.

And suddenly, Brendan had an idea.

* * * * *

The ride operator had returned with a new set of keys a few moments after he'd stormed off. Michael Evans and his friends left, and before they did, I heard Michael chuckling darkly about somebody in the Freak Tent.

I had arrived at the front of the line. The operator, who was even sweatier from his journey across the carnival, extended a large jar that I dropped a handful of change into.

"Riding alone?"

"Yes."

"Enjoy."

He pulled open the door of the gondola and ushered me inside. When I sat down, I felt something wet seeping through my pants and realized that I had sat down in some spilled cola.

I was about to ask the ride operator if I could have some extra time at the top, but before I could, he was already gone. I could feel the wind brushing through my hair as the gondola lifted off the ground and rose higher and higher in the sky.

All around me, there were lights. They were so beautiful, just like they'd always been. The stars were beautiful, too. The gondola came to a halt about halfway to the top, and when it did, I realized that these lights were going to be the last things I'd ever see. The operator was going to be the last person I'd ever talk to. The gondola railing was going to be the last thing I'd ever touch.

The ride started turning again. For a moment, I leaned over the side of the gondola to try to see as many things as I could. I touched everything and even started to talk to myself because the ride operator was such a stranger and it made me sad to think that my final words were to him.

When I gazed at the crowd of people beneath me, I hoped that Simon had gone home. I didn't want him to see me when I was all messy on the ground. I didn't want anybody to. I just didn't know where else to do it because no other place was as special to me as the Ferris wheel.

When the gondola rocked to a halt at the top, I kept my eyes on the sky because I knew that if I looked down at the ground, I would be afraid.

I wasn't sure how much time I had before the ride started moving again. All that I knew was that I didn't have much. The first time I tried to stand, I couldn't find the strength. The second time, I wobbled to my feet and inched my way toward the gondola doors.

"Tommy?" I asked quietly. "Are you here?"

I waited for a sign... anything. I waited to hear his voice or feel his breath against my neck. I spread my fingers, waiting to feel his lace between mine.

But there was nothing. I was alone.

"Tommy?" I repeated, turning around. "You said you'd..."

But my voice trailed off to silence and suddenly, I was afraid again. I was afraid because if Tommy wasn't here, then where was he?

The longer I stood there, the more it all made sense.

Tommy Swanson was dead. I saw them take his body away five years ago. He couldn't be here and he never would be. Tommy Swanson was *dead,* so why did I keep feeling like he wasn't?

Or maybe he's here, I thought to myself, *and I just can't see him. Maybe he's standing right beside me. Maybe he never left five years ago.*

"I know you're real!" I called. "I'm not crazy, Tommy! I *know* it! Show yourself!"

Silence again. I felt my body begin to shake. I started shaking so badly that the entire gondola began to shake, too.

"YOU SAID YOU'D BE HERE!" I roared. "YOU PROMISED ME!"

I heard my voice echo back at me. I realized, then, that I had to do this alone. I squeezed my eyes shut and opened the gondola doors.

"Just… just do it!" I told myself. "Just fucking *do it!*"

But my feet wouldn't move.

"It's just one goddamn step! Just… just *take that step!*"

As I struggled to lift my foot, I cursed Tommy Swanson for lying to me. I cursed myself for being so weak and I even cursed my mother because I had been searching for a sign to live and she didn't give me one.

I squeezed my eyes shut and prayed for the second time outside of church. I prayed for a sign. If I had just one, I wouldn't do it. I'd sit back down and I'd ride the Ferris wheel to the ground and run away in search for a place where the stores still sell green face paint and people pay for it with green dollar bills.

"Give me a sign…" I whispered. "*Anything.*"

But nothing came. The night was quiet and empty, so I opened my eyes and made up my mind that I was going to be strong for the first time in my life and I was going to do it. I started counting down and the the closer I got to zero, the lighter I felt.

"Five… four…"

I thought about Susan Smith. I thought about Harold Stacy.

"Three… two…."

I thought about Brendan and his father.

"One…"

And lastly, I thought about Tommy Swanson and when I did…. I was not afraid.

I slackened my grip on the gondola railing and I leaned forward.

"Tommy…" I whispered, and when his name left my lips, I was ready. I was ready for the pain and everything that would come after.

But as I stood alone on the Ferris wheel that night, I heard something. At first, it sounded like a whistle, but the longer I stood there, the louder it became. All of a sudden, I heard a loud bang and I stumbled backward.

Boom!

When I opened my eyes, I could see *green*. The large firework sparkled in front of me for a moment before disappearing. Afterward, I heard more whistling and this time, a firework collided with the gondola beneath mine and exploded all around me. The dozens of green sparkles were so close that I felt like I could touch them.

It brought me back— back to the days when Brendan and I would sing songs on the swings and play hide and seek in his attic. The air suddenly smelled like the apple pie my mother used to make before she became sick. For a moment or two, I wondered if heaven smelled like childhood and if it did, then I must've already died.

Boom! Boom!

The sound— it reminded me of how the fireworks used to rattle the picture frames in the hallway. It reminded me of the night when Brendan and I climbed onto the roof to watch them. Earlier that day, I waved to Harold Stacy while riding my bicycle around the neighborhood and ate cereal during cartoons and the milk was sweet and sugary and Susan Smith wasn't on the back of the carton.

171

The fireworks began late that year. Brendan was worried that they weren't going to shoot them off that night.

"Do you think they forgot about the fireworks?" he asked me.

I laughed. "No way! They're probably just... waiting for the perfect moment."

And as I said it, a large firework exploded in the sky and Brendan's eyes lit up.

That day was so long ago. But as I stood there, atop the Ferris wheel, more fireworks exploded around me and that day felt *closer*. After several moments, I laughed. I don't know why I laughed, or even how, but I laughed and tried to catch the glittering bits of green as they danced in the air around me because I wanted to keep them forever.

It's strange, isn't it? Fireworks are one of the few things that always look the same. They look beautiful when you're nine years old and just as beautiful when you're ninety nine.

Boom! Boom!

I kept hollering and jumping and dancing between the green fireworks. A few times, I closed my eyes and prayed. That was the third time I ever prayed outside of church. I prayed that Brendan was watching them, too.

For a moment, when I opened my eyes, everything was green. The sky was green, my hands were green, and as I looked out at the trees around the carnival, they were green— even if only for a moment.

"I've never seen something so beautiful," a voice beside me whispered.

I pulled my eyes away from the sky, and when I did, I saw Tommy Swanson sitting beside me. At first, I thought he was watching the fireworks, but after a moment or two, I realized he was watching me.

His eyes twinkled. "Just beautiful."

"You kept your promise," I said, so relieved that my tears stopped falling. "You're *here*."

He chuckled. "Of course I'm here, kid. What kind of person breaks a promise? Now, do me a favor and return these. I don't know what came over me. A boy like me's just got sticky fingers, I guess."

He tossed something into my hand— a set of keys. At first, I was confused. Moments later, I realized they belonged to the ride operator.

"It was you," I said, my voice filled with wonder. "You stopped the ride."

"At just the right time, huh? Maybe it was just a coincidence. Or maybe it wasn't."

His eyes fluttered over to mine. Then, he winked— the same wink he had given me on the playground the morning after he died. All my life, I thought I'd just been seeing things, but when Tommy winked at me at the top of the Ferris wheel, I knew that I hadn't.

That was his *sign*. When I was nine-years-old, Tommy Swanson gave me a sign that things were going to be alright. Now, as we stood in that gondola atop the Ferris wheel, somebody else was giving me a sign…. and I had a feeling I knew who it was.

Suddenly, the ride rocked back into motion. I let out a cry and grabbed hold of the railings before collapsing into the seat. I watched as the small gondola doors rattled closed.

Tommy sat down beside me. He outstretched a hand. "How about I keep my promise and hold your hand on the way down?"

Before I could answer, he grabbed hold of it. For a moment or two, he squeezed so tightly, I could've sworn he was about to break my fingers. When I felt teardrops on the back of my hand, I realized he had started crying.

"Don't cry…" I whispered, worried that it'd make me cry again, too. "Please…"

"Christ, kid," he said, wiping his eyes. "You must think I'm such a goddamn baby."

"Please don't cry," I repeated, trying to keep my voice steady, but as the words left my lips, I started to cry, too. We both cried and held one another as the Ferris Wheel drew closer to the ground and our ride came closer to its end. I'll never forget that night and how warm his hands felt against mine. I'll never forget the feeling of his breath against my neck or the places where his tears touched my skin.

"Tommy?"

He wiped his eyes. "Yeah?"

After a few moments of silence, I managed to say what I'd always wanted to... since the day that I tied flowers around the monkey bars and he came to me in my dreams. It scared me to say it, and I'm sure it scared him to hear it, but as the gondola continued to lower, I managed to choke out, "*You have to go.*"

Go. The word echoed in the open air.

He didn't turn to face me. "You want me to go?"

"You have to *leave.* Be *happy.*"

When I said that, he swallowed hard. "I know I do, Hunter."

And that moment, I'd never been more scared for anyone in my entire life. As the gondola approached the ground, I wondered...

What happens to boys like Tommy Swanson? Where do they *go*?

As I wondered, I closed my eyes and prayed for the fourth time outside of church. I prayed that somebody, somewhere, could save Tommy Swanson. It couldn't be too late for him. That was my fifth prayer— that it wasn't too late for boys like Tommy Swanson to be saved. He saved me, but why wasn't anybody there to save him?

Tommy could feel my tightening grip. "Christ, kid," he laughed through the tears. "I said I'd hold your hand, not *give you* mine..."

I didn't laugh or loosen my grip. Instead, I closed my eyes because for some reason, I thought that maybe the moment would last longer if my eyes were closed. Maybe the moment would never end and we'd never have to say goodbye.

But the moment didn't last forever. Moments can't. They die, too. Just like people.

More fireworks exploded in the sky and when I looked over at Tommy, he was still crying and looking down at the floor. Even when I nudged him, he didn't look up. I tried to give him a noogie because that always made Brendan laugh, but when I did, Tommy kept crying.

When I looked over the gondola railing, I saw that we were only teen or fifteen feet off the ground. Panicked, I exclaimed, "Watch the fireworks with me!"

I kept repeating the same thing over and over, and the closer we got to the ground, the more hysterical I became.

"Watch them with me, Tommy! Look at them! They're beautiful, aren't they? Watch the fireworks with me! Come on, watch them with me!"

I tugged at his hand in one final attempt because we were almost on the ground. The fireworks kept bursting in the sky above us and I realized all I've ever wanted since I was nine years old was to watch the fireworks with Tommy Swanson.

Before I could stop myself, I became angry. I don't know where it came from, but I knew that the anger had always been there. If Tommy hadn't been sitting with me, I would've screamed. I would've punched the side of the gondola until my knuckles were bloodied like Gabriel's because no matter what I did, I knew that I would never be able to watch fireworks with Tommy Swanson and it wasn't *fair*. All these years, I just wanted to be with him and laugh and look at our reflections in the funhouse mirrors, but the world took that away from me.

"Tommy," I said one final time, all the while, trying to swallow the anger. "Won't you please watch them?"

He finally looked up. "I don't need to, Hunter. I see fireworks every time I look in your eyes."

175

Boom! Several more fireworks expanded in the night sky. The green light looked so beautiful across Tommy's skin. The gondola finally rocked to a halt and the ride was over.

"I kept my promise," Tommy said, trying to smile through a few final tears. "I held your hand the entire way down. Now, it's your turn to keep a promise for me."

I looked up into his eyes, which were round and bluer than a summer sky.

"What is it?" I asked, my voice barely a whisper.

He leaned in and kissed my forehead. "Promise me you'll live a long, happy life."

And then, Tommy Swanson was gone.

The Night Tommy Swanson Crossed Over

Where is Tommy Swanson? He never returned after that night on the Ferris Wheel. I wish he'd send me another sign— so that I could know that he's happy wherever he is. What is he seeing? What does it *look* like?

Something changed in the neighborhood that night. I can't really explain what happened, but it stormed so terribly and almost all of the mulch washed off of the playground and onto the street.

Across the neighborhood, Jackie Swanson was having a slumber party with a few friends from school. I'm not sure when it happened, but one of the girls told me that they were all awoken in the middle of the night because all of the old toys in Tommy's room lit up and started making noises— from the rocket ships to the wind-up robots.

When Jackie opened the door to Tommy's room, she screamed. When the other girls tried to calm her down, she cried, "Are you…. are you *here*?!"

* * * * *

After Tommy Swanson disappeared that night, I stumbled my way off of the gondola and onto the carnival paths. The dirt was soft and I could feel the bottoms of my shoes sinking into it. It was strange feeling dirt beneath my feet when I didn't think I'd ever feel it again.

I removed the key that Tommy had given me from my pocket and tossed it at the ride operator's feet.

"Found this on the seat," I mumbled, keeping my head down. I don't remember what he said next, because I wasn't even listening. With my head hung low, I headed past all of the tents and toward the tree lining along the edge of the carnival. When I got there, I slipped through the tree lining and between all of the red leaves and branches.

"Brendan?" I called, peering through the darkness.

When there was no answer, I said it louder and louder until I was screaming it.

That's when I heard his voice. "*Hunter.*"

And I saw him through the leaves. He was standing in a clearing and we were both so far into the trees now that the leaves were green.

We didn't talk, we just kissed. We kissed and it was so wonderful and I wish that everybody had somebody to kiss like that because kisses can change you.

Brendan's kisses changed me that night.

Do you remember when I was at the corner store, buying my mom powder for her bruised eye? Do you remember what I said? I said that *moments* change you. Terrible moments can stay with you and nothing can ever make them go away.

Although I still believe that, I'd just like to let you know, wherever you are, that there will be new moments. There will be moments when you hold his hand and kiss him in a beautiful place surrounded by fireflies and white flowers. And those moments are perfect. They're so perfect that they make living through all of those other awful moments somehow... *worthwhile.*

I wish I would've known that five years ago. Maybe if I did, something would have woken me up the night when Tommy Swanson was fifty feet away from me on the playground. It might have been a bad dream or the sound of his crying. I could've looked out the window and I could've seen him on the playground. I could've ran outside and stopped him— just in time.

I wish a lot of things, you know? I wish childhood never had to end and that Brendan's dad never had to leave us. But most importantly, I wish my 9-year-old self could've known what I know now because

178

maybe if I did, Tommy would still be alive. I could've changed his mind or maybe, if I was just a little bit too late, I could've held his hand while he died.

I wish that more than anything. He died alone that night—holding his own hand, and whenever I think about that, I cry because I was *right there*. I was so close. I could've held his hand so that he felt a little warmer or a little safer. I could've told him everything was going to be okay and that he shouldn't be afraid.

I don't know. Maybe I'm crazy. I just wish for that, you know? I wish things could've been different the night Tommy Swanson died.

Made in the USA
Lexington, KY
03 January 2019